He Threw the Stone into the Sea.

The riseing was almost full, and it floated for an instant, then sank, staining the water an awful blue. He turned with his hands at his side, ready to die.

"Damn you!" Tese shouted. "Take up your sword and fight. You have no right to die like a king!"

"I have no sword," Kemen said. "Feed me to the sea and have done with it. Help me, my kinsmen, to die." He held out his empty hands.

Tese howled and ten kings moved forward as one, a hungry beast with teeth of blades.

In spite of himself, Kemen was afraid. He stumbled backward a step, into the water, and something brushed his foot. It felt like a hand but wasn't. He looked down and saw washed up on the smooth, gray slab (for the wyrld was too new for sand) the sword of Noese. He thought for a moment he was going to weep, but his face danced like water and all that came was a mad laugh.

He took up the sword and scattered kings like leaves.

had ever lived since time began. Each sat with

Terry Bisson

WYRLDMAKER

A Heroic Romance

Fowler's Books
Buy - Sell - Trade
323 N. Euclid
Fullerton 92632
or
2634 W. Orangethorpe
Fullerton, 92634

A TIMESCAPE BOOK
PUBLISHED BY POCKET BOOKS NEW YORK

Another *Original* publication of TIMESCAPE BOOKS

A Timescape Book published by
POCKET BOOKS, a Simon & Schuster division of
GULF & WESTERN CORPORATION
1230 Avenue of the Americas, New York, N.Y. 10020

ISBN: 0-671-83578-5

First Timescape Books printing July, 1981

10 9 8 7 6 5 4 3 2 1

POCKET and colophon are trademarks of Simon & Schuster.

Printed in the U.S.A.

*For Judy,
Still the One*

WYRLDMAKER

ONE

KEMEN OF PASTREYN WAS OLD FOR a young man but young for a king in the eleven small kingdoms of Treyn that were strung like beads on the path at the bottom of the wyrldwall at the warm end of the sea. He had no queen to tell his stories to but he had a son, a boy named Hayl with hair as white as cutsjark shell. And there lies the end of one tale and the beginning of another, for they pass this same place like rings on the water that, in fleeing, reveal where the stone went in. They shall both be told.

But first, some killing.

"Why does the wyrld have a wall? What makes the sea move?"

Kemen didn't answer Hayl. Taking his son by his still-narrow shoulders he turned him around so that his bare feet scraped loudly on the gravel floor, and with a comb made from a whale's grin

combed out his long hair for the three braids a
boy must wear to his first ordering.

Tear, the boy's old nurse who had been the
king's old nurse, looked on lovingly, leaning her
broad back against the sparkling mud and mica
wall, patiently waiting to begin the intricate
plaiting that only she knew.

"What makes the sea move?" Hayl asked
again, smiling mischievously.

"The sea does not move."

"It does! It wiggles in the riseing. Why? And
do I get to wear swords to the ordering?"

"Of course. Now hush." Kemen cuffed the
laughing boy, then pushed him toward Tear,
who began plaiting his braids. Questions.
Kemen liked answering them even less then he
liked asking them, and Hayl knew that. What
Hayl liked was teasing his solemn father.

A few more riseings and Hayl would be a man.
Already he was taller than Tear, who made him
sit on a sleeping turtle's back while she bent
over him, working the proper ribbons into his
braids: white, to show that his mother could not
braid his hair (though he did not know why);
green for the fourth, the second oldest, house of
Treyn; yellow for boy.

Kemen's own hair had been braided long ago,
and ribboned three riseings past all in green for
king. He pulled on his fringed ceremonial robe
of weed and skin, as pale and red as the sky, and
paced the narrow shell and tooth walled room,
watching Tear work and listening to her sing.
Kemen filled the room like a ship in too small a
sea. His calves below his robe were as corded
and as thick as the sinewy trees that grew to the

edge of the water at the other end of the wyrld, where there was wood. His great arms were bare, for only women and wyzrds wore sleeves, and thick from oars and battle. He had been handsome once. Now his high, proud face was hard, used-looking, etched with the thick lines of war and the deeper, finer ones of exile and loss. His black eyes were big, but neither bright nor deep.

Tear finished and Hayl stood up. In his simple yellow weedcord robe, he looked like any other young prince of the Treyns, except for the startling white of his hair—and his eyes, which were as blue as a wyzrd's.

"You look a prince," said Tear, her old eyes shining as she adjusted his robe, "now act one. This ordering is more important than you are entitled to know . . ."

"Now you hush, old woman!" Kemen said. He crossed to the inlaid cabinet of tooth and shell where his own father's braids were kept, and opened its smallest drawer. He took out the two blade-hangers and tied one around Hayl's waist and one around his own. They were of soft sea leather edged with shell, and each had three loops sliced whole from the spine of a white sword lion.

On the wall over the cabinet hung twenty swords in six sizes, all of dull pink surfhorse shell. The largest three were nicked and thin with war; Kemen left them hanging. He selected the three next-to-smallest swords and slipped them into the loops of Hayl's hanger. The boy's face gleamed.

Tear straightened her own old, rough robe.

Her smile of pride and hope was the only fine thing she owned, and Kemen was glad for it, even though he couldn't force himself to return it. He knew that her joy in what was to be settled at the ordering was as great as his own despair. So be it. The wyrld had seen enough of war, his hall of emptiness, and his heart of dreams.

"Let's go," he said, ducking out the doorway.

Hayl ran eagerly. Kemen paced him with long strides and Tear scurried along behind. They followed the smooth slab at the edge of the waveless sea until Kemen's low hall was far behind them and they could hear the murmur of the ordering in the high hall of all the Treyns ahead. Their steps were long; already they could feel the lightness in their feet from the rising that was laying its soft fingers across the wyrld.

The murmur turned into voices as they approached the hall. Kemen could feel the doors of his heart closing, one by one, with each step he took.

"You didn't bring your swords!" Hayl said, looking at Kemen's empty hanger with alarm; then at his eyes. Hayl looked away from the emptiness he saw there, and pulled one of his own swords from his hanger. "I will protect you with mine," he said, laughing again, cutting skillfully at the still surface of the sea.

Kemen caught the small sword by the blade and twisted it from Hayl's grasp.

"The sword is for the ordering. Not for killing, but for show," he said angrily. "A sword for killing I could never hold like this."

He gave the sword back, clenching his fist to hide the thin line of blood across his palm.

"Now come. We are late already."

The blue wicker hall was loud with kings.

And not only kings: wordbearers, the wyzrd, the waterjudge and her four blind husbands as prescribed by law, the bonecarrier with her splendid, vacant smile; all were in, or near, their places. The guests were few, but valued; there had to be guests at the ordering that decided the sequence of the boats of Treyn when the riseing lifted them from sea's floor. Two of the gloomy Nove, whose trade fed on Treyn's life-crowded nets, sat whispering, each cluching its one claw in its one hand; a boat preparer from the clear end of the sea stood behind them, singing drunkenly, resplendent in its scales and fins; and across the broad hall, three of the greasy-winged Alo, the cloud-walkers that came from the sky but never returned to it, chattered noisily through their glass-toothed grins.

But loudest were the kings. They stood in a clump at the center of the hall, strutting and posturing under the glowropes, passing a skull of cold fish wine and fondly caressing the long blades that gleamed in their hangers, hanging down almost as far as their knees.

There were ten of them. Some were scarred and bent with war, for the Treyns had been engulfed for three riseings in a bloodsome wedding war, and the two kings who had fought had coaxed allies from their cousins and kin; but all were robed now for peace, in their heaviest and

most intricate gowns, for this ordering was to
see an end to that war.

Splendid in their polished fins and furs, they
laughed and joked loudly, old men passing
the sour wine to older enemies with a wink,
younger men squeezing the hand they had tried
to slice away not two sleepings before. Prince-
lings and children dodged yelling between their
legs in rowdy games. Around them the hall was
crowded with all the peoples of Treyn: boat-
pullers and net pullers, breakers of stone and
shell, and the musicians talking of the songs
they would use to coax the fish from the reef
when the riseing raised the boats from the
harbor floor. Foodsellers wandered among them,
hawking sweet pieces of beings warmed between their great, soft hands.

All waited for the last of the kings to arrive. All
waited to witness the surrender that would end
the war. All Treyn waited to witness the throwing of the bones that would order the boats in the
lightening that was already causing the blood to
dance, the children to leap higher, and the kings
to gesture as they talked as if their hands had
wings.

Then the wait was over. The last, the young-
est, the most wild, the fiercest and most sorrowful of the kings of Treyn appeared.

The hall fell quiet. Kemen stood in the weed
arched door, with Hayl at his side and Tear
lurking behind them like a shadow. Kemen
turned slowly, pretending to study the crowd, to
show that his hanger was empty of blades. Then
he walked across the room and joined the crowd

14

of kings, leaving Tear but taking his princeling with him.

"So," said Tese, the one-armed king. He grinned with his teeth and handed Kemen the skull with his only hand. Kemen looked into the hate-stormed eyes of his enemy and drank deep. It was bitter.

It was done.

"So," he said, and passed the skull on around the circle. Another enemy. A friend. An enemy's friend. . . . The talk and the jokes started up again. The surrender had been accomplished, noted and unremarked, as was proper: Kemen had accepted the bitter wine from his enemy, and had drunk from the skull of the Grandmother without his blades. The great hall of Treyn grew noisy with joy.

Lose a war and gain a queen. Kemen forced himself to look to the end of the hall where iinkRe, Tese's daughter, waited naked under her robes to become his bride again. Her eyes were small and bright with victory. Kemen tried to smile and, giving up, looked away. As the wyzrd began to rattle the bones, he pulled Hayl closer to his side, like a lucky charm.

As always, it was always a wyzrd that threw the bones; as always, a sigh went up when they rang across the great table, carved from a single shell; it was Treyn's time of hope and promise in the wyrld.

But this time the sigh turned into a gasp. Then a groan. Then curses, low and then loud.

iinkRe was the first to scream. Kemen was struck silent with horror and, for one foolish instant, hope.

The wyzrd grinned.

There on the table, among the time-cleaned bones of the Grandmother, a blue light gleamed; familiar, for it had begun all the wars and sorrows of Treyn: the blue stone of the woman called the blue stone Woman.

Hayl grabbed it before anyone else could move.

Kemen grabbed it from Hayl. What did the boy know of all this? he wondered. Kemen had told him that his mother had died and been peacefully eaten at sea; yet Hayl's face showed triumph, not confusion. The stone was so cold in Kemen's hand that he closed his eyes in pain. The hall fell quiet as death.

Then Kemen heard the warlike scrape of shell on stone, the slick whisper of a blade being pulled. He opened his eyes and saw Tese's face knotted with anger, Tese's blade raised, ready to strike.

It was Hayl who struck. He slashed with his miniature sword, carving a circle of flesh from Tese's knee. Kemen caught Hayl's arm and, surprised at his own strength, pulled him off his feet and threw him over the heads of the kings. Hayl flew, light in the riseing, almost to the ceiling: then down, spinning and screaming, in a long slow arc into Tear's arms, who caught him easily, for the riseing was gathering its first fullness. With a last angry look at Kemen, Tear ran with the boy out the door.

A sword cut Kemen's arm and he jumped back, startled by the brightness of his own blood.

"Kemen has shamed me enough!" Tese shouted. "Help me shame him with death!"

It was war again, but now it was only Tese's war. The other kings held back.

Kemen took another cut on the same arm, then parried the next with a hastily-grabbed club of bone. Tese's men joined him from the corners of the room, drawing secret knives from boots and belt, for only kings came armed to the ordering. Kemen cracked two shins with his club, then split a head like a melon.

Then his club shattered.

Tese fell back, aghast at the sight of the ruined bone of the Grandmother in Kemen's hand. Kemen staggered, horrified at what he had done. iinkRe screamed from her prison throne. The nine other kings raised their swords as one; now it was the war of all against one. Kemen had shamed Life itself.

With the blue stone burning his hand with its coldness, Kemen threw the splintered bone into Tese's face and broke for the door, knocking two kings down into a shouting pile of limbs and robes.

"Kemen of pasTreyn . . ."

He stopped. He knew, somehow, that it was the wyzrd that had called his name, even though no one in all the Treyns had ever heard a wyzrd speak before.

"Kemen . . ."

Kemen turned just in time to see Tese lop off the wyzrd's head with one swift, angry slash of his blade. Still holding his sword, he hurled the head across the hall.

"Kemen of pasTreyn . . ."

The wyzrd's head was still talking as it sailed, spinning, through the air; but it had nothing to say but Kemen's name. He caught it by the greasy, unbraided hair, surprised to see that there was no blood; the stump of its skinny neck was as dry as a cut root. "Kemen . . ." Kemen didn't want to hear what it had to say. He set down the wyzrd's head as carefully as if it had been a bag of walkfish eggs and hurled himself out the door, still clutching the cold blue stone that had returned to shatter his life again with hope and horror.

Hayl and the old woman were gone.

It was never dark in the wyrld and never bright, never cold and never warm. At the time of the riseing, when two men weighed half what one had weighed before and the reed boats floated to the top of the water, the sky's dull red sometimes dimmed a little, and an extra glow rope might be hung in a windowless hall. But the difference was slight. The wyrld was always much the same: the red-gray sky boiling overhead, glowing, sending down thin fingers of mist to touch the waveless sea indifferently.

Kemen ran along the water's edge, his feet in the still-heavy water. His hand was cold and the blue stone glowed between his fingers like a smaller, brighter sky of blue. He stopped, out of breath. Behind him he could still see the bulk of the great hall of pasTreyn, a giant mass of mud and reed and shaped shell, towering three times as tall as a man, rising amid the used-up boats, trash middens and low huts of the central village of the Treyns. Ahead of him, around the slow curve of rock and sea, was his own hall, with the huts of his musicians clustered around it; and beyond that, another hall and more huts. Behind them all rose the sheer rock face of the wyrldwall, disappearing into the misty ceiling of the sky. In front of them all was the gray-green, waveless sea, rising to marry the mist in the near distance. That was all. It was a small, a closed wyrld, without spaces or corners or places to hide.

Kemen heard shouts and cries behind him. Although he could see no one, he knew it was Tese and the other kings—all of them now—preparing to come after him. Every soul in all the Treyns was probably helping them sharpen their blades and fasten the difficult buckles on their shields, for who could defend him now? He had broken the bone of the Grandmother. A wyzrd had called his name. He had savaged the kingdoms with a senseless weddingwar; then failed even at his own surrender! He decided to stop running. He waited with his feet in the water that was just beginning to dance in the riseing, and held the stone that was too cold to hold without hurting, and hurt, and remembered . . .

He had been a young man. Six riseings ago he had stood on the grass mound beside iinkRe, his father's brother's daughter, her teats bared in the banns for the wedding that was to seal the peace and assure the generations as the generations had been assured since time began. The wordbearer stood between them, and behind her the wyzrd, and on either side of the two kings, Tese and Esliv. Esliv was already an old man, but a happy one: for he had lost many sons and wives to the sea, and had almost despaired of seeing his line passed on until this ceremony. He smiled on his son and two kingdoms smiled with him. Kemen smiled too, though he couldn't remember why; he could remember very little of what had happened to him before what happened to him then: it was as if he had been born there, grown, whole, wondering and waiting on the grass-mound between the sea and the wyrldwall, surrounded by the ceremony of his own wedding, when the woman rode from the sea.

Even the wyzrd was smiling, almost cracking the paint that covered the moles on his pointed, papery cheeks. Kemen remembered the wyzrd best, for it was the wyzrd that had seen her first with his shrewd and tiny eyes. Just as the ceremony was completed he clapped his wrinkled hands and pointed out over all their heads.

She was riding out of the water on a clear pony through which Kemen could see stones and weeds and sea. She turned the wyrld blue around her: she held the blue stone out before her in the palm of one long hand as if lighting the way, and ever since she had been called the blue stone Woman, even by those who were not there and did not see her the one time she appeared in the wyrld.

The crowd parted and she rode through it to the grass-mound.

She was long-limbed and blue-eyed and dark behind her skin, not pearl-colored like the musicians and their kings. Her hair hung loose in a way not fitting for a woman. It was long, and as

20

white as what Kemen would come to know in the sorrows she brought him as snow.

But the strangest thing of all but one (for the wyrld itself was the strangest of all) was that she immediately spoke his name: "Kemen of pas-Treyn."

iinkRe screamed, for they had just been wed and the wedding would not bind if another woman spoke Kemen's name before their flesh was joined.

Kemen jumped onto the pony behind the blue stone Woman. He laughed. It was a new sound in his throat.

The pony leaped.

Tese howled like a seal trapped in a cave and drew his blade and slashed his new son across the face. Kemen twisted the sword from his new father's grasp and cut with it once, leaving an arm flopping joylessly in the long grass, missing both its sword and its body.

Esliv wept.

They rode off, not looking back, and she told Kemen her name was Noese. The pony was swift. Its hooves rang like bells on the path at the foot of the wyrldwall, with a music that Kemen felt could call the fish from the sea's very stones. Even the blood from the cut on his brow tasted sweet. He laughed again, then laughed at the sound that laughter made.

The riseing was upon the wyrld and the reeds were beginning to rustle and stand, and they stopped at the notch in the rocks where lovers went to hide from the wyrld when they had agreed to stop hiding from each other. Instead of grazing on the tiny leaves, Noese's pony turned to water and flowed away between the stones. Kemen was amazed and tossed Tese's sword away.

"Noese . . ." he began, but she placed her finger across his lips and laid the blue stone on the ground. With her long fingers she closed the cut across his brow, then laid aside her sky-striped robe and with her body taught his body how to sing.

When he awoke she was gone. Beside him lay a long sword so bright that in its blade he saw his face for the first time in his life, and he was afraid.

The handle itself was longer than an ordinary shell blade, almost half the length of the sword. It was fashioned of a hard, dark substance like black bone, inscribed with no design, and the blue stone was set in the end of it, big as a baby's fist, cold with a glow that pulled at Kemen's eyes as if it were farther away than anything in the wyrld could be, even lying in the crushed reeds next to his still-sweet-smelling hand. He took it up. It took two hands to hold it. Mad with loss and rage, he stumbled through the reeds, look-ing for Noese, but she was gone. He looked behind the rocks and then around the wyrld, but it was as if she had never been.

In every street and kingdom of the wyrld—and there were kingdoms all around the curve of the sea—Kemen hoped to see the flash of her hair ahead of him. He expected every stream he crossed to turn into a pony, and leap. Even after he gave up, he kept on looking. He shipped as a flenser of eels on the low, flat boats of Malk, and learned to grumble with the other men; he learned to warm food in the bellies of fresh-killed whales, and gaped with the crowd in Anker as the cloud-walkers glided in on their skin sky boats with baskets of bright metal called knives that rang like the sword of Noese. At the far end of the wyrld, where the sea was cold, he learned what wood was, and killing too. Forgetting he was meant to be a king, he hired in small wars, and learned that the sword of Noese made a killing song in his hand. It gave power to his arm and filled his heart with a cold, fierce joy that fed on men.

He learned war, for warriors are what wanderers must be.

He saw the wyrld but he never saw Noese again.

After he had been gone three riseings he sickened of both love and killing. He knocked the blue stone from the hilt of the sword and traded it to a wyzrd in ooN for a pair of boots. Walking to the end of a pier, he sheathed the great sword in the sea and then walked back around the wyrld, to home. He had nothing to show for his sufferings but the scar across his brow.

In his father's hall he found a white-haired boy.

No one could say where the child had come from. He had appeared, naked and smiling, in Kemen's cold wedding bed, only ten sleepings before. But Kemen's old nurse, Tear, had known somehow that he was his father's child, and had clothed him and named him Hayl.

"Father," Hayl said, and took his hand.

"Where is my father?" Kemen asked the old nurse.

Tear backed away, unwilling to embrace him.

"Gone up the wyrldwall, three risings ago," Tear said bitterly. "The smokebeaks have been fed. He is dead and you are king."

The kings were closer now. Kemen heard the clatter of sword and shield, the ring of boots on stone. He didn't look around. Let it end, he thought. The blue stone felt as cold in his hand as a dream. Since his return, for three bloody risings, he had warred with Tese, pretending anger at his father's death, but it had all been a lie. He had fought because the price of peace was iinkRe, and he had been foolishly saving his bed for Noese, for he thought he had seen her again, peering out at him from the boy's blue eyes. He had grown to love his son, even though dreading his questions, walking with him between battles, the great hand curled around the small one like an Ythri around its shell. Dreaming. How many had he dismembered, and how many more sent to die, lusting after a dream? Now let it end. A stone is not a woman.

He threw the stone into the sea. The riseing was almost full, and it floated for an instant, then sank, staining the water an awful blue. He turned with his hands at his side, ready to die.

"Damn you!" Tese shouted. "Take up your sword and fight. You have no right to die like a king!"

"I have no sword," Kemen said. "Feed me to the sea and have done with it. Help me, my kinsmen, to die." He held out his empty hands.

Tese howled and ten kings moved forward as one, a hungry beast with teeth of blades.

In spite of himself, Kemen was afraid. He stumbled backward a step, into the water, and something brushed his foot. It felt like a hand but wasn't. He looked down and saw washed up on the smooth, gray slab (for the wyrld was too new for sand) the sword of Noese. He thought for a moment he was going to weep, but his face danced like water and all that came was a mad laugh.

He took up the sword and scattered kings like leaves.

TWO

THE BLUE STONE SWORD WAS THE color of whatever eye peered into the broad flat of its blade, and its thirst for blood was deep. It was not like the yellow knives used in the wars on fish and men that lost their eagerness so quickly that a warmaker had to carry four in his sash hanger, as well as a stone to remind them how to kill. The blue stone sword reminded men. Half again as long as half a man, it cut the air with the dreadful sound of widows whispering; light in the hand, it was heavy when the killing was done, even in the riseing that was beginning to raise the rushes up from the mud and the boats from the bottom of the sea.

It was heavy now. The killing was done and the kings of Treyn that had lived had dragged themselves away on the stumps of the limbs left behind. Kemen was unharmed. He wiped the sword on Tese's robe, shaming the ornaments of peace with still-bright blood, while Tese's eyes regarded him mournfully from his head where it lay discarded nearby. Kemen hung the sword in his sash and walked off toward his hall. His heart was heavy too, but he knew the worst was yet to come.

Tear was waiting for him on the low, worn step. "Gone," she said.

"What?" But already he knew.

"Hayl is gone." The old woman stood up and attacked Kemen with the broad sides of her fists. "You killed him. You and your endless war and magic stones!"

"How?"

"I dragged him back here screaming. He wanted to fight alongside you at the ordering; he's as mad as yourself. I sent him to his room and heard him screaming back at the kings howling along the shore. Then he grew quiet and I was afraid. I ran in, and he was gone. See for yourself."

Hayl's room was empty. His ornate small bed looked as if it had always been empty, like the false egg of the wheeled snail that did not reproduce but was created anew each riseing. His swords and sash hangar lay neatly by the pillow. His three robes were hanging on horns on the wall: sky-red for princeling, weed-blue for son, yellow for boy. Kemen gathered them all in one arm and held them against his cheek, which was as dry as the floor of a cave. He envied the old woman her sorrow.

He didn't bother to call out or look for Hayl. He knew he had gone, and he knew now what he had to do.

He folded the robes and laid them across the

bed. He picked up the small swords, still hung in their sash, and left the room. While Tear watched, he crossed the common skin-roofed court to the inlaid chest and replaced the sash, then hung the swords back on the wall for some other princeling or some other king. He opened the largest drawer in the chest. There lay his father's braids and his father's father's braids, and more, coiled tightly like thinking snakes. The tiny knife that lay across them was cut from a single jewel-like tooth and useful only for the killing of kings. He used it to cut off his own braids and laid them across the others, then shut the drawer.

Already there were voices outside, murmuring like new water.

The riseing was stabbing at the wyrld, then withdrawing, making it hard to stand. Tear carried a basin from the outer hall, her face a mask. Kemen laid aside his robes and began to wash, slowly, preparing the smokebeak meal. When he was finished he sat for a long time and dried before he went out.

All of pasTreyn surrounded the door to his hall. They gasped when they saw the huge strange sword he carried with the dread blue stone in its handle. Musicians and fishers, boat-formers, children and lovers ripe in the rush of the riseing, swaggering boys and oldlings dark with sorrow: they fell in behind him and followed as he walked toward the great hall where the dying robes were hung.

The hall was littered with broken benches and splintered bones—the remains of the ruined ordering. Kemen walked in alone. The white robes hung in a line on the wall, like the ghosts of kings not yet dead, and he took one down with the tip of the blue stone sword. It was customary for the old king's closest companion to help him put it on, but Kemen was not old and he was alone. Even Tear had waited outside, her arms folded across her heart as if guarding it.

It was a sleeved robe and felt strange across his shoulders. He belted it with a rope of weed and turned to go, and saw that he was not alone: at the high end of the hall iinkRe sat in the bride's chair, her face as still as the sea. "Have you seen my father?" she asked. Her eyes looked forgotten.

Kemen hurried out the door, and faced the crowd that waited there.

"Rejoice," he said, "your king is dead. He stained the water with the blood of his people. He broke the bone of the Grandmother. The wyzrd called his name. His rule was war and horror. He broke the peace of the kingdoms for . . . a dream. Now he is gone, and you behold the smokebeak meal. This sword which has eaten of kings . . ."

He held it over his shorn head.

". . . I take with me, for the sea will not take it, nor will the wyrld."

Kemen walked alone past the low walls and shard piles to the foot of the wyrldwall and started up the path kings walked to die. No one followed him even that far. Who would mourn a king who had traded his kingdom for a place in the arms of a stranger? His step was heavy, even in the riseing. He had failed even at dying correctly, for he had lied. He had not done it all for a dream. He had done it because lust had sung to him and he had taken it for love.

Only one watched him go: old Tear. She sat below a wall at the edge of the village and watched not the king but the boy he had been. She watched until he disappeared into the sky, and she was found soon after, her big heart stopped at last, by a child on some childish errand.

Dying felt good. With slow, measured steps, Kemen trudged up the narrow trail, even though he could have leaped in the riseing and climbed the switchback like stairs; he cherished the vivid pain of the sharp stones on his feet, the chill of the first clouds hanging like weeds from the sky, savoring these parts of the final ritual as if they were life itself.

The trail that took the kings away was steep and narrow, a switchback carved from the solid, mossy rock of the wyrldwall. There was a wide spot far up, right before the trail was lost in the swirling mists of the sky; it was a good place for kings to stop, and look back on the wyrld they were leaving. The Treyns were laid out below in all their small beauty, nestled in the quiet curve of the sea. The low forests of reeds were trembling in the riseing, straightening up from the mud like blue dancers after a rest. Near the great hall, the musicians and fishers of Treyn were gathered on the shore, watching as the reed boats that only remembered to float in the riseing popped majestically to the surface of the sea, disturbing the water with huge waves as high as a hand. Laughing gangs hooked the boats in. Girls on errands took long steps, and even oldlings tried a leap or two in the riseing, when a child could carry the bundle two men had cursed before.

It was Treyn's time of joy, when the wyrld made the promises that were to be redeemed with flesh on reefs far out to sea, when the ritual songs were played that convinced the fish it was time to die.

If Kemen had looked, he would have seen the musicians, polishing the great blow shells, but he didn't. Generations of kings had stopped here for their last look at the wyrld, but Kemen didn't stop. He plunged on up the path, into the sky.

Dying felt good.

The sky was a soup of mist, laced with light and loud with scurrying sounds. Rockrat and leam, glowing insects and others never named were thick in the life-soup of the sky, living on the plants and moss that were said to live on the blood of kings, just as the giant smokebeaks that were half flesh and half cloud were said to live on small animals between kings. Kemen walked carefully at first, trying to avoid the creatures dodging between his feet, then gave up, trusting them to dodge him. He held the sword out in front of him, but the stone lighted nothing but itself. He dragged it at his side, remembering that every generation of Treyn had climbed this path without it.

He couldn't see the path at his feet through the mist but he could feel it growing narrower, until it was no more than a crack in the stone. His steps grew heavier as he climbed away from the wyrld and the riseing. The sky grew quiet and there were no more scurrying sounds.

Then he heard why. He heard the great, dismal honking of the smokebeaks ahead, and he knew, for the first time, pure cold fear. He was entering the short circle of life. Soon he would see wings larger than boats, see the flash of beaks greater than doorways, know death's darkness.

Kemen knew the place even though he'd never seen it; knew he was approaching it even before the path began to widen and level. The clouds themselves opened for it, and when he saw the dying field he recognized it just as the foamling knows the stone that broke its egg, searching it out and swallowing it when it is time to sink and die; he knew it from the memories of all the kings that had gone before him, for nothing was lost in the world. Life was a soup, bitter and thick, and now Kemen's memories would join the others, washing down with blood and mist from sky to sea.

Even his memories of the blue stone Woman.

The end of the wyrld was a ledge as large as the stripping deck of a cutsjark boat, twenty long steps from end to end. At one end, cut into the stone of the wyrldwall, was a door that looked as if it had never been opened. On a stone bench beside it six figures sat, all in white robes, without heads. Kemen could see by their long fingers that they were nothing but bones. He sat down beside his father, at the near end of the bench.

Here in a row were all the kings of Treyn that had ever lived since time began. Each sat with the treasures of a lifetime between bone-tipped bone feet: a jeweled bell, a glass tooth, a baby's dagger. Between the feet of the last one lay the rain-colored singing shell that had stopped singing the day Kemen's mother had died eight lightenings before. Kemen laid down the sword beside it and closed his eyes. He was ready to die but he didn't want to see the smokebeak that ate the heads of kings like grapes and spat out their souls like seeds.

He was shivering and he heard a great horn sound. Then a nasty clackering. His eyes crept open and he saw his feet, still covered with flesh, and between them his doom and his treasure: the sword. In the broad gleam of the blade he saw shadows moving in loops and he looked up; the smokebeak was straining to form out of the mist, the scaled neck and dead orange beak becoming more solid with each sickening lunge at his soft, sweet head. He felt it like a whisper of air around his neck, becoming more solid with each pass.

Wings painted the sky with darkness. Kemen clutched his hands between his legs to keep them from grabbing the sword. He closed his eyes again and smiled in spite of his terror. The circle was joining around him. He was able to die. He felt his soul curl up and smile in the darkness of his breast, like a woman waiting for a lover who is certain to arrive soon. The great jaws clacked over him, almost solid now, smelly and fetid like water.

They tore at his neck and he grabbed for the sword. . . .

There was a long terrible scream which Kemen thought was his.

But it wasn't.

He opened his eyes. The scream had been the scream of the door opening. A shape in a brown robe stood in it, beckoning to him with a sleeve. Puzzled, he got up. Behind him he saw the smokebeak hovering off the ledge, gathering for its feast, its single eye quivering like a dish of gray jelly, its beak snapping at the cloud-thick air.

The robed shape grabbed his arm and pulled him through the doorway with fingers sharp as sticks. "I am dead," Kemen thought, but he was wrong. He looked back and saw that the bench was empty where he had been sitting. Horrified, he realized that he was carrying the hated sword, just as the door shut behind him with another scream. The circle had closed with him outside it.

It was the first time Kemen had ever seen darkness; then there was a burst of light. A small, fierce creature danced before his eyes, clinging to a stick like a surf monkey. It was made of light and behind it Kemen saw a stairway littered with dung and bones, leading upward.

Kemen backed up against the closed door. The robed shape waved the stick to which the creature clung.

"This is fire," it said.

THREE

FIRE WENT FIRST, FOLLOWED BY the robed shape which held fire out before itself at the end of a long sleeve. Kemen followed without being asked. He dragged the sword behind him, its tip ringing dully on the stone steps. He carried it by the end of the hilt near the blade; the other end, where the stone glowed, was too cold for holding comfortably, and he was afraid of the feeling it gave him of power and killingness. He would rather be afraid.

It was a long climbing. The stairs were dark and steep, winding upward between damp stone walls. At long intervals, in bird skull holders fastened to the walls, were sticks like the one fire clung to, but each was blackened at the end and gave off darkness rather than light.

As the stairs climbed through the rock in long, slow turns, Kemen felt himself growing heavier, leaving the wyrld and the riseing behind. Perhaps he hadn't failed at dying after all. He was content to follow, step after step after step. The only sounds were the scraping of the sword on the stone, and the crunching under his feet of skulls too small to ever have housed a dreaming mind. Once he stopped to rest. The robe and fire ahead of him made a soft sound, like a rug being dragged from a room. Then there was total silence and darkness as they disappeared around a curve.

Kemen didn't like the darkness. He hurried after them.

They were gone.

The stairs ended at another door. It was ajar and edged with light. Kemen pushed it open and stepped through.

He was on a narrow ledge with the sky below him. It looked the same from above as it did from below: smoky, boiling, red and talkfish gray. The wyrldwall encircled it as a pot encircles a soup, and he could see clearly to the other side of the wyrld, where the wall of streaked stone rose out of the mists to a smooth, unbroken rim. The other side of the wyrld looked close enough to touch, even though Kemen knew it was a journey longer than boats last across the sea that lay hidden below.

Another sky was above him. This one was light gray, streaked with long parallel lines of light, and it looked cold, motionless, and incredibly far away. Kemen didn't like looking at it.

He was tired and hungry. The ledge was narrow and led nowhere. Fire was gone, and the stick it had clung to lay blackened by the door. Next to it was a carefully folded robe.

The wyrldwall itself ended just above his head. By laying down the sword and stretching upward, he could reach the top with his fingertips. Then he could pull himself up and see what was on the other side. But he didn't. Instead, he wrapped himself in the robe and lay down and slept. The robe smelled like old rooms.

When he awoke everything was as it had been before. He was still hungry. He closed the door that led into the wyrldwall, then folded the robe and tossed it over the top. He tossed the stick after it. Then the blue stone sword. Standing on his tiptoes, Kemen hooked his fingertips over the top and pulled himself up, and saw another wyrld, more strange, more awesome and more vast than anything he had ever seen before.

Everything in this wyrld was far away. From the edge of the wyrldwall it sloped in a mammoth gentle fall to a great bowl-shaped plain of gray rock streaked with red dust and crossed by jagged blue lines, like scars. On the far side, so far that it hurt his heart to look across to it, the plain was rimmed with giant mountains. Far below, at the center of the plain, white clouds were clustered like the sheep that fed near the sea; isolated clouds drifted in a long line up the far side of the plain to clothe the lower slopes of the mountains in white. They were the only things in the wyrld that moved.

Here was the most of anything—distance or wyrld or air—that Kemen had ever seen, and it filled him at once with terror and longing. His eyes were pulled to the mountains, which gleamed blue-white above the clouds, then gray at the fin-like peaks. They were so high, and so far, that it seemed they would tip the wyrld with their hugeness as a trapped whale will rock a boat when it rolls to one side, and Kemen stepped back involuntarily as if to balance things. His limbs felt heavy here, like the wyrld between risings, like battle after losing blood.

He left the stick behind. He wrapped the blue stone sword in the robe to make it easier to carry and started down, into the wyrld, toward a nearby village he hadn't noticed before.

The town was one wide street paved with dust and stone, between low buildings of shard and red rock that had neither roofs nor doors. Kemen looked over the walls and saw that they were not huts but bins. One was filled with unfinished leather, wide skins dark with hair. One was empty, another stacked with flattened, slab-like wings, bloody at the root. Others held lumber, huge rounds of rope, bones sorted by size and shape. There were no people or beings of any kind: no shouts, no smells. It was a village rich with silence, and Kemen was certain that perhaps he was dead after all.

He walked down the street to where it ended, where the village faced on a vast sea of wyrld without water. A stone pier pointed across the plain to the mountains like a finger of bone. He turned and walked back. There was one building in the village with a door: a hall twice as tall as the others, with walls of smooth mud broken by narrow windows. He was about to go in when his hair was seized from behind by a hand, while another reached around him and held a serrated stone knife against the hollow part of his throat, where it was at its very softest.

"The robe," a dry voice whispered.

For the first time since he had climbed the wyrldwall, Kemen smiled, for what did he, a dead man, have to fear from death? The hilt of the blue stone sword was cold under the robe that hid it. He held it out and a man stepped around him, still pressing the knife against his throat. He was taller than Kemen and thin, as if his dry, papery skin were stuck directly to his bone. He had no hair or lips. He snatched the robe . . . uncovering the great sword that became a blur in Kemen's hands as it sliced through the wrist that held the knife as easily as an oar goes through water the wrong way.

The man screamed. He fell to his knees and jabbed at the dust with his stump, while he covered his lidless eyes with the one hand he had left, as if he were afraid to see the one he was looking for. He was wearing a short, filthy, dust-colored robe that cracked when he moved. He found the hand with his stump and screamed again when he realized he had nothing to pick it up with.

Kemen laughed, and his laugh sounded harsh even to himself. "You like the knives, then, but not the cutting?"

"I was sent by the wyzrd for the robe," the man whispered without looking up. "I thought you had stolen it."

"Wyzrd? Where?"

The man looked up into Kemen's eyes for the first time. His slate eyes were empty of hate or pain or fear. His new stump was barely bleeding, oozing thick dark drops that fell heavily into the dust. He pointed with it to a low hill beyond the edge of the village of bins. At the top, in what looked like a pile of trash and rock, a rounded window gleamed.

"The robe stole me," Kemen said.

He retrieved it and left the man studying his own hand in the street between his knees.

If wyzrds could be said to live the wyzrd lived in a low circular house of yellowed glass and yellow stone, joined and patched by battered timbers. The hill was steeper than it looked, and Kemen's legs felt heavy and stiff in this wyrld where there was no riseing. There was no path. The hill was almost flat on top and the area around the house was littered with glass and bones, scraps of thick rope and giant ruined wheels.

Dragging the blue stone sword in one hand and holding the brown robe in the other, Kemen circled the house until he found a door.

He felt as if he were awaking from a dream, in that empty moment after the dream has fled and before the wyrld has rushed in to fill its space. He was not dead. He did not know where he was, or why, but he knew the wyzrd might know. He knocked and the door swung inward.

The ceiling was low and formed of ribs of wood. The floor was dirt and the mud walls were hung with picture rugs. The wyzrd sat on a bone-legged bench by a window of smoky glass, looking out at the awesome mountains across the wyrld.

Kemen held out the robe, but the wyzrd shook the back of his head without turning and said: "It is the sword of Noese I want."

The sword of Noese!

When he turned he looked like all wyzrds, his face white as if with powder or death, his white hair waving weakly on top of his head when he shook it. His small eyes, enclosed in neat wrinkles, were bright blue and his mouth appeared only when he spoke. He was wearing a simple white leather robe, with pieces of fur stuck to it, and long sleeves. If he had stood, he would have reached only to Kemen's waist; but sitting he seemed to fill the whole room. He had that rich musty smell that Kemen had always thought was old rooms and sea but knew now was wyzrd.

"The sword of Noese," the wyzrd said again.

Kemen handed it to him, shuddering. It wasn't hearing the wyzrd speak that alarmed and thrilled him; he had even expected that. It was hearing her name. It was the first time he had heard it since she had told it to him, deep in the reeds at the foot of the wyrldwall. He had never spoken it even secretly to himself.

Laying the hilt across his lap, the wyzrd reached up to the wall behind him and took down a tooled skin and bone sheath. Even though it was only half as long as the blade of the sword, the sword went into it easily, as if it were folding in on itself. Then the wyzrd held it between his knees and placed both his tiny,

43

wrinkled hands on the glowing stone at the end of the hilt. A look of pain turned to peace across his face.

"So cold in its coming," he said.

The bench where the wyzrd sat was the only furniture in the room. Kemen laid the robe he was carrying against the wall and sat on it. He had a thousand questions, but he didn't know where to start.

"You know this sword?" he asked finally.

The wyzrd laughed. "You think it's you I've waited for all these changes of the wind? No. This is the sword called Wyrldmaker that you bear, rising from the sea where it has lain hidden. I wait for it but it does not wait for me. It is hers."

Kemen gulped and said her name. "Noese. You will . . . give it to her?"

The wyzrd laughed again and pointed to a bowl of meat and seeds under the bench. Kemen had lost track of when he had last eaten, and he wolfed them down, even though the meat was old and sickening, while the wyzrd said what he had dared not hope to hear.

"You will give it to her," the wyzrd said.

"I?"

Again the wyzrd laughed that wyzrd laugh. He pointed with one yellowed finger toward the mountains that rose like a jagged wall at the far end of the wyrld, then swept his arm around the wyrld, around the room. "Somewhere beyond all this lies the city called Llamp. It is there that you must go, bearing the sword called Wyrldmaker to Noese, who is called Wyrldmaker too."

Kemen felt a thrill surge through his body.

Death was behind him now. Noese lay before!
He stood, and reached for the sword.

"Not yet," the wyzrd said. "Not yet." He
clutched the stone in the hilt to his shriveled
breast and smiled and closed his eyes.

Kemen watched him grow older: his sagging
face stretched over the small bones of his skull,
his eyes sank in his head like divers after one
last treasure. Clutching the stone that made his
fingers glow blue, he mumbled peacefully.

"Drink. Sit. I expected an old man. Time is as
filled with wyrlds as the wyrlds are filled with
time. I have waited long, and now I seek my
destiny . . ."

"As I seek mine," Kemen interrupted impa-
tiently.

"You have none!" the wyzrd said sharply.
Then he fell to mumbling again. "Only hers.
Remember that and you will be disappointed,
but not destroyed. Tell no one of the sword you
bear."

He mumbled on but Kemen wasn't listening.
His mind was filled with thoughts of Noese.
Against the wall of the cornerless room he saw
two boots in a pile of belts and knives and robes.
They were of stiff leather, a little tight, but he
managed to pull them on. He had a journey
before him. He slept.

When he awoke the glass in the window was
rattling like teeth. The room was darker and the
wyzrd was dead. The plain through the glass
looked dim, as if someone had drawn a reddish
veil across it. The mountains were fading away;
they disappeared as Kemen watched. There was
a howling noise all around.

Kemen pried the wyrldmaker loose from the wyzrd's cold fingers. He hung it, in its sheath, on his rope sash and turned to go. To Llamp!

Outside, the walls of the wyzrd's house were shaking. Kemen ran down the hill and into the street of the village. Harsh red clouds filled the air. He found the man who had tried to rob him in front of the hall with the door, where he had left him. His stump was almost healed.

"What is this moaning?" Kemen asked. "What is this tearing at my robe and hair?"

"Wind," the man said. "The wind is here and soon the fleet will come."

FOUR

THE HALL WITH THE DOOR WAS AN
inn, either half-finished or half-destroyed, and
Kemen moved in and stayed while the ·bone
fire smoked and the narrow windows high
in the wall shook as if in terror at their wyrld
becoming wind. Wind moaned. Wind screamed.
It howled until Kemen's ears were indig-
nant with its dry, idiot shout, and the distant
mountain rim and the awesome plain and
even the bins directly across the street had
all vanished behind a red wall of dust and
sound.

The inn was empty. The door was at one end
of a long, dark and drafty room; a fire smoldered in a pit at the other. Stacks of beams and
broken stairs were piled on the floor, as if the
hall had once been finished and divided into
rooms and floors, but had been gutted. The
fire gave off neither heat nor light. It was

slowly built, and then more slowly tended, while Kemen slept then woke then slept again, by the thin man who had tried to take the robe; he was still the only living being Kemen had seen in the village. With his one hand and one stump, he dragged in great pitchy bones and curved beams, pushing them into the guttering flames unbroken. Slowly, the fire grew.

The thin man never spoke unless he was spoken to, and Kemen only spoke to him once, to ask him the name of the village. It had none. More even than the wind, that terrified Kemen, and he was impatient for the wind to die so he could begin his quest and leave this strange half-wyrld where things were not named.

As the fire grew larger and the wind grew stronger, the man dragged a pot from under a pile of rubble in a corner of the hall, and slowly began filling it with water, dark liquids, fur, hides and animals, all brought from outside, some still alive when they went in. Kemen could hear cries from the soup as it cooked. He ate from it only when his hunger grew painful. Once he found an entire hand, curled as if pleading, and threw it back.

The rest of the time he waited. He sat in the corner of the inn farthest from the stinking fire, wrapped in his robe against the chill, gnawing a bone against his hunger, drowsing against boredom. He played with the sword called Wyrldmaker, amazed that its blade was as long as his leg, yet slipped easily into a sheath shorter than his forearm. He stared into the stone. He dreamed of Llamp, of Noese and reeds. He waited.

But the wind didn't go away. It stopped rising and Kemen got used to its constant low moan, but the streets outside remained empty, the houses shut, and he couldn't imagine how he was supposed to continue what he now saw was his quest and find Llamp.

"The fleet is in!"

The door was banging in the wind. But there had been no door before. Kemen awoke from a dream to find that he was no longer alone. The inn was filled with men and women, animals and beings of every description, carrying weapons and packages, shouting greetings and curses to one another. The soup was boiling on a leaping fire, strings of fat slaves were being snapped to rings even as they were being hammered into the wall, smells and jokes filled the air.

The door had been built while he slept; now lofts and ledges were being fastened to the walls by webbed and winged workers, and tables and chairs were being roped together out of board and bone.

Kemen went outside. The wind had not died but it seemed wounded; its howl had dropped to a low moan, and the air was clearer, as though some of the dust had finally found the surface it had been seeking. Kemen's dream had been of deep and silent things and he stood stupefied in the now-busy street, watching the crowd of beings heading for the bins with goods and toward the inn with treasures and clothes. Some were winged, like the Alo of the wyrld he had known, but armed and with fiercer eyes. One he saw was furred and striped; another with a lizard's head dodged through the crowd. But most were men or women like himself but older, more worn, with arms or legs missing under their shabby robes; their eyes were small and red and set in wrinkles.

They were all coming from the pier at the end of the street. Kemen worked his way against the crowd to see what had happened, his heart beating excitedly.

Two great ships were already tied up at the pier. Two more were appearing out of the wind-clouded plain, their house-high wheels booming over the rocks, their streaked slat and skin sails rattling and shaking. Kemen had never seen such machines. He had seen, and even sailed on, the shell-fleet of the Mord that traversed the still seas of his wyrld; but those were swift and delicate vessels, splendid with bloodpaint and drawn by petulant jelly-horses. These ships were huge cities on wheels. The largest, approaching the pier, was longer than the village itself and its barky masts were twice as tall as two towers. It changed shape as it turned and slowed, creaking and groaning as its huge ropes and timbers slid and snapped with the strain. Its flat, sideless deck, strung together of rope and hide and misshapen boards, was crowded with red-eyed men.

The pier was piled with stacks of hide and wood and glass. A cry went up from the crowd as the larger ship ground into the stones, crushing a woman and the serpent she had been planning to sell into a single stain. The heavy sails fell with a clatter into loose stacks on the deck. The name of the ship was carved into the blunt bow: Corec. Another cry went up as the smaller ship, behind it, began to crash to a halt.

Kemen turned back for the inn, to begin seeking passage for Llamp.

"Llamp. It's on the wyrld's bottom."

"No, it's at the top."

"Llamp. Like warwings, a story to scare children with. Begone. I am a man with locksheep, stone and rope to sell, fine rope!"

"Llamp, where wyrlds kiss instead of lovers. . . ."

"Llamp. Speak to me instead of Lightwell, or Relres where it is easier for a man to fly than walk, for I circle the wyrld with the wind and if Llamp were more than wyzrd's talk I would have passed through it many times."

A long table had been built, fitted with long benches, and Kemen sat with the windsailors and traders as they came and went, and questioned them. He learned many things, but he did not learn where Llamp was. He sought out and spoke with all who came: windmen from raw rimwyrld towns with an eye, or an arm, or a half leg missing; noisy giants in birdfur robes with single, expectant eyes; hollowboned beings from wyrlds without weight—for he was learning that there were wyrlds on wyrlds on wyrlds.

Kemen learned that this village with no name was no village but a warehouse, an outstation in an outland among outwyrlds, a place of no consequence; a wide spot in the fleetpath that circled this wyrld's rim, where the ships that called with each windrising put in for repairs and provisions, and traded leather, glowing stones, fur and rope and slaves among themselves.

He learned to his sorrow that Llamp was a myth. It was a varied and sparkling myth, of rivers of ice and forests like seas and a city taller than it was wide, but no more real than an oldling's love song, and his heart sank.

Then he learned to his joy that his own wyrld, too, was a myth to the ones that sailed the wind. To them, nothing but the circle they traveled was real; there were neither cities nor wyrlds beyond the fleetpath worn by their ships' wheels, except for the three far cities in the center of the plain, marked by clouds, that none of them had ever visited, called the Cities of the Well.

He learned that none had ever visited them because it was a one-way trip, for no ship could make it back to the rim from the deep center of the bowl-shaped plain. It was a journey as dangerous as it was long, across a landscape cracked by stormlines and prowled by eumen and eating hills.

Then he met Mone.

At the dark end of the table, away from the fire, sat a mournful white hillock of a man with a ring on each fat finger. He ate noisily from sea-green bowls, served by a grinning warrior in chitin armor who was attached by a long chain to a scowling woman. Kemen had approached

him to question him about Llamp, but had been
turned away rudely by the flat of the warrior's
sword; angered, he had kept his own sword
sheathed and gone on about his business, which
was far more important than fighting.

Kemen heard laughter and looked to the end of
the table. The warrior was yanking at the chain,
which went from his swordbelt to a collar
around the woman's neck. Choking, she spat at
his face. He thrust the bowl at her, but she
refused to take it and fill it; instead, she cracked
it across the crest of his narrow helmet. The
onlookers at the table howled and shouted for
more as the dark, stinking soup ran down the
angry warrior's face.

The fat, white man looked up briefly, then ate
on from the bowl already in front of him.

The warrior wiped his face, then drew his
sword. The woman pulled to the end of the chain
as the warrior pulled her to him, wrapping the
chain around his fist link by link. He held the
sword at the level of her neck, whipping the tip
in tiny arcs as she was dragged nearer.

At the last moment she ducked under the
blade and, in one swift movement, palmed a
meat knife from the table and threw it, spinning, into the meat of his thigh that was exposed
between the slabs of the warrior's armor.

He howled and pulled it free.

Fast as she was with a small knife, the warrior
was faster with his broad sword, and he swung it
with a butcher's easy skill. Kemen leaped to his
feet as the inn fell still: so still that only the
nasty whine of the warrior's blade was heard
over the wind as it slashed the woman's robe

open in one precise cut, leaving a thin line of bright blood down her chin and between her heavy breasts. Just a warning.

Then with the point of the sword the warrior pinned her ear to the wall.

"Kill her," said a voice from the crowd at the table.

The fat man went on eating.

The warrior laughed as the woman screamed and tried to pull away, the blood trickling from under her reddish hair, onto her neck and her shoulder. His laugh began triumphant, then turned to a low gurgling sound as his teeth closed across the cold blade of the Wyrldmaker that had entered one of his unshaven cheeks and exited the other.

The warrior dropped his sword and the girl pulled free.

"Kill him," said a voice from the crowd.

Kemen shook his head and held his outstretched arm very still. "Let him move and kill himself."

The warrior's teeth were clenched in a rictus grin on the blade; he couldn't turn to see who or what had pierced him without tearing his face open. Only his eyes moved in wide circles of rage, until the woman had been thrown a rag to bind her ripped ear. Then Kemen pulled the sword free in one swift motion, and the warrior turned to see who had gored him. Retching, he spat out a piece of his tongue, picked up his sword from the floor where it had fallen and walked out into the wind.

The inn was still while Kemen slipped the sword that was half again as long as half a man into its short sheath; then the room burst into a storm of excited talk.

Kemen was breathing hard with the exultation of war. The fat man looked up from his soup.

"You seek Llamp?" he asked. He said his name was Mone.

Kemen sat at the end of the table with Mone, who had the smallest eyes Kemen had ever seen, and the roundest, the most surrounded by soft folds of fat. They were blue. His fine robes were all colors, made of a soft cloth that shimmered like knives.

"I'll be honest with you," Mone began. "I was not bound for Llamp until I met you. Great treasures wait there, but even greater dangers lie on the way. Yet . . ."

Kemen nodded hopefully.

Mone's eyes fell to the blue stone at the end of Kemen's sword. He smiled and Kemen saw that he had no teeth, only gray gums like a baby seal.

"Yet you are worth four of the one you pierced! I happen to have a treasure that, to sell in Llamp, would gain me the world were I so bold as to go. And with you at my side I would be bold! Sign on as my warrior and I will take you to Llamp."

"Yet the windsailors say there is no such place . . ."

"If the truth were known, they are fools and liars," Mone whispered. "Coenti Jjl, where the windships sail, trades with Llamp. Were the wind not risen, I could show you Coenti Jjl, sparkling like a jewel under the meteor scarred peaks of the Mountains of Aer, all the way across the wyrld. It is there that we sail, and from there a fearsome journey that few know, and fewer still, survive. One which, to be truthful, I never before now would have dared . . ."

Mone's voice dropped and his rings flashed as he beckoned Kemen closer.

"I see by your face that you have made a worthy decision, for if you were not man enough to go you would not be the man who *could* go. Now. Tell no one where we are bound. Wait here, watch the fire, and when three more beams have burned join me aboard the *Corec*."

He rose to go with an easiness that belied his bulk. He pulled at the woman's chain, and she followed him, her rag pressed to her ear. While Mone paused to adjust his shimmering robes, she leaned toward Kemen and whispered: "I . . ."

"Do not thank me," he said with a smile. "What I did, I did only because it was right."

"I wasn't going to thank you!" she hissed. "And for that reason. I was going to ask, did he promise to take you to Llamp?"

Kemen stiffened and looked away. The woman stumbled as Mone pulled at her chain, and both went out, into the wind.

While the three beams burned Kemen enjoyed the toasts of the windsailors who had witnessed his swordplay. The wine was good, and it was good to be admired. The sailors soon had Kemen flushed with praise, until one warned: "You have not seen the last of Misk." She was an old woman with a cocky, toothless grin.

"Misk?"

56

"The one whose teeth you brushed with steel. My name is Frduae and I have sailed with him. He is a bad one. He seeks revenge as weight"— Frduae dropped her curved knife, decorated with wild scenes, so that it stuck in the table— "seeks wyrld."

FIVE

COREC WAS AN EIGHTEEN WHEEL-
er with masts that whipped like swords and
booming sails of slat and scale and skin. Travel
was like war. The sails, the deck, the ship itself,
all were being constantly destroyed and then
repaired as the ship lurched and rumbled
through the wyrld. As many builders as sailors
were in the crew, and so many were crushed
between the timbers that each shift was called a
dying and each new one saw another missing
who had fallen from the rigging or been ground
to meal in the smoking axle shafts.

Once started, the great ship never stopped. It
lumbered along the stony fleetpath at half again
the speed of a running man, followed by flocks of
large-headed beasts called sneke that fed on the
bodies and parts of bodies that fell or were
tossed over the side. The sneke never stopped
either. Delicate eaters, they paused only long
enough to snap off the lips or the fleshy part of

the thigh from the bodies thrown to them, then ran after the ship in a panic, squawking as if afraid of being left behind, scrambling between the low bushes on their orange pads.

Mone lay below the tallest of the three branched masts in a narrow cabin, wrapped in a rug with a scented rag over his tiny nose, continually eating from a silvery bag. Kemen stayed on deck and watched the sneke, and watched the stones rush past. Beyond them, there was nothing to see. Reddish clouds enveloped the ship and the fleetpath, and Kemen wondered if the wyrld he had seen before was only a dream: the vast plain with the clouds at the center and the awesome mountains called Aer at the other side.

The woman was called Maer Ash. She told Kemen that and nothing more. Though she was attached to Kemen by a chain no longer than a room is wide, she avoided speaking to him as if he were her captive, and one too foolish to notice. They sat side by side, but each alone, under the rearmost creaking mast. Sometimes they were joined by the old sailor who had warned Kemen of Misk, Frduae, who was too weak to work and too stubborn to die. Frduae loved to talk. It was she who pointed out the ships that passed, who knew their histories and destinations and crews, even though they were no more than dark shapes in the dust. It was she who pointed out the villages as they passed them, even though to Kemen they appeared to be nothing more than blurs that might have been piles of rocks.

It was Frduae who told them of the eating hills

that moved across the plain below, that were much feared because what they ate was ships. She was telling them of the eumen who fed men, in pieces, to ponies, when she was interrupted by a scream.

Kemen looked aloft. The wide sails were turning, shearing the legs off the sailors who clung to the mast so that they fell to the deck in a kicking pile. The ship lurched, turned, tipped on half its wheels with a splintering sound, then righted itself.

"What is this?" Kemen asked.

"The turning," Frduae said. "The place of no coming back. We just turned off the fleetpath and are headed down the wyrld."

Kemen looked out, over the side of the *Corec*. The wind had dropped and was hitting them sideways now, full in his bewildered face. The darkness was beginning to lift as the dust slowly cleared. The wheels boomed over naked rock.

"Down the wyrld?"

Maer Ash laughed for the first time since Kemen had met her. It was a harsh sound. "He told you we were going to Coenti Jjl, didn't he?"

Kemen nodded.

"All ships go to Coenti Jjl, you fool. All but one. You're on the oldest ship in the wyrld, taking its last voyage. You're on the one ship of the fleet that is bound down off the rim, across the plain, for the Cities of the Well!"

"You didn't know?" said Frduae, scornfully. "Do you think if I were a young woman I would be taking the voyage from which no sailor returns?"

There was another scream as a goat-footed

man from some far wyrld fell from the rigging and was smeared on the stones by a wheel, but Kemen wasn't watching. Dragging Maer Ash after him, he ran below and shook Mone out of his stupor. The fat man sat up, shamefaced and sorrowful.

"I'll be honest with you," he said. "I lied. It's not my only fault, but it's my greatest one."

Then he fell back to sleep.

The wind dropped but the *Corec* never slowed as it rolled down the wyrld. For sleeping after sleeping and dying after dying they crossed the red stone slab, smoked through pools of deep dust, plunged between stone cliffs. Always in front of them, visible now that the wind had dropped and the air had cleared, were the clouds far below that marked the Cities of the Well.

Kemen's limbs grew heavier, then lighter, varying with each turn of the ship as it careened through the steep, broken wyrldscape. The plain was vast but far from smooth. They were far below the fleetpath now, and though they sometimes passed other ships, they were wrecks: ruined, empty of life and even of bodies. There were no more blurs that might have been villages, no beasts, no low bushes. Even the sneke had been afraid to follow. Even the dust.

He had been deceived—but knowing that, Kemen found that he really didn't mind. Maer Ash was more friendly now, having proved him a fool; Frduae was filled with terrifying stories; and Noese would be found somehow. Kemen held the sword called Wyrldmaker across his knees, like a promise, and watched the emptiness roll by under the light-streaked sky.

"Look," Frduae said at the end of one long dying. Her jauntiness was gone and her face was pale. Her voice was shaking as badly as her bony hand. She pointed to a bluegreen line that crossed their path far ahead. "See that stormline," she said. Kemen had never heard fear in her voice before.

He found out why as the stormline rushed nearer.

The bluegreen was gnarled trees. *Corec* never slowed but plunged into them, shattering branches and trunks against the hull. Kemen's stomach lurched upward, then his feet; he held onto the railing with one hand and onto Maer Ash with the other, for all his weight was suddenly gone. The broken trees were flying upward, away from the wyrld; then the ship itself was in the air, trading ends in a slow, sickening spin.

Maer Ash screamed, but no sooner had she paused for breath than they were across the awesome crack in the wyrld that the trees had covered. Kemen had looked down into it, and then covered his eyes. *Corec* hit with the sharp sound of splintering wood, reeled and righted itself, then sped on as sailors flew from the masts and smashed like soft eggs against the stones. Kemen's stomach was back; his feet hit the deck.

One giant wheel had broken off, and Kemen and Maer Ash watched it roll off between squat, ashy hills. Frduae struggled to her tiny feet, cocky again and surprised at being still alive. She pointed behind them at the shattered trees, spinning slowly higher and higher into the air.

"Could we but stop we would be rich," she said. "See how the stormwood floats! In the Cities of the Well it is more precious than life itself."

That remark puzzled Kemen, for it had never seemed to him that life was precious at all.

On they rolled. The wind dropped but the wyrld grew steeper and the great ship never slowed. Now they could see the lights under the clouds far ahead that marked the Cities of the Well, and it seemed to Kemen that they were falling into them. Every other direction was up: the wind-scoured rim behind them, like a streak of red smoke; the meteor-scarred mountains called Aer far ahead and far above, so high, Frduae bragged, that flesh turned to leather on the passes; the light-streaked sky.

They were falling. Kemen liked falling, and he sat with Maer Ash and Frduae until Frduae went below to sleep in her nest of friends, and then he lay with Maer Ash in a rug Mone had left them, and slept, the chain collapsed between them.

Kemen had the strangest dream. He dreamed as always of Noese and reeds, but this dream was more real. They made love as they never did in dreams. They were falling. It was the sword. Noese took it within her, without the stone. Kemen took the stone in his hand, without the sword, then the stone took him within itself, like

Noese, like wyrlds. Hayl gave Kemen the sword, then cried as Kemen pulled him from the brown-tipped teat. Hayl was falling. Kemen reached for him but it was too late; his loins exploded wet with light as he missed: it was her hand he caught. He had never dreamed it was so small! It fit within his own like Hayl's, and both fit between her breasts like shell in shell in shell.

But it was Maer Ash's hand Kemen held between Maer Ash's breasts. He was awake. She was awake too and her eyes were close to his, like little green seas.

"Who are you?" she asked.

Kemen decided to tell her.

He felt shaken. He stood up and pulled on his robe, then tied on the sword called Wryldmaker that had lain beside him. He walked to the edge of the pitching deck and when the chain pulled taut she had no choice but to close her robe and follow him.

"I was once a king," he said. "Now I am a man with a sword more powerful than himself, on a mission he does not understand. I was having a dream. I miss my son and I think I dreamed I killed him. I am a warrior afraid of his own sword. There. I have never told anyone before."

He studied her face and said, "I know you think me a fool."

She smiled. It was the first time he had seen her smile without laughing, and it was sweet.

"I do," she said.

They watched the wyrld roll by. Kemen's breath came back and the weakness left his knees. No one was on deck but themselves and the bird-faced Poplei who steered the ship, whose faceted eyes saw too far away to walk, and who could only ride a ship or fly.

"What is it that you fear?" Maer Ash asked.

"Magic. There is too much magic about it all. Look." He pulled the sword from its sheath and stuck it in the deck. The blue stone shimmered in front of his chin. He took it in his hand, cold, and turned it and it came loose, just like in the dream. The sword looked dead without it.

Leaving Maer Ash standing beside the sword, he walked to the end of the chain and tossed the blue stone into the air. There was a brief flash of light and what came down into his hand was the sword itself, with the stone in the hilt. The sword in the deck by Maer Ash had disappeared.

"This is no ordinary work you are about," she said.

Kemen shook his head and smiled, not proudly but resignedly. He sheathed the sword and joined her again at the rail of the rumbling ship. His knees felt weak again. "That is why I am afraid. Now, who are you?" he asked, touching her hand.

She pulled it away. "I am exactly who I seem."

They lay back down in the rug, being careful not to touch this time. Kemen was not sorry he had told her but he felt uneasy, as if he had betrayed Noese, even though he had not mentioned her name. He tried to remember his dream but couldn't. He felt as if he had been crying, even though he knew he never wept.

As soon as Kemen saw it he drew the sword called Wyrldmaker, then as quickly sheathed it

66

again and joined the others who stood at the rail of the *Corec*, watching with a fascination more hopeless than terror, for the thing they saw was too monstrous to fight.

A hill was moving into their path. It grinned whole cliffs, chasing ponderously after the ship as it swerved; the upper slopes of stone flowed hideously like brittle water, the lower ridges quivered and snapped; it filled the air with great hollow screams as if movement were pain unforgiveable and death the punishment the ship would bear.

"The eating hills," Frduae said. "We are finished."

The helmsman, a nine-foot Moidor with blackened stumps where his wings had been removed, tugged at the wheel that turned the wheel that turned the ship. Wheels split on stone as *Corec* heeled over and scraped the lower slope of the hill, smearing it with reddish streaks that marked where men had hit. With a huge shudder, the ship careened off, just as a ridge became a claw and snapped off two of *Corec*'s three masts and fed them to a cave. Kemen, Frduae, and Maer Ash fell into a heap on the deck as the ship righted itself and hurled on down the wyrld.

Kemen was surprised to find Maer Ash's hand nestled in his own again. She didn't pull it away so quickly this time.

"We escaped!" Kemen said, but Frduae shook her head. "We are ruined," she said, almost proudly.

Behind them, while they watched in horror, the hill was digging at its slope with one of the masts, dropping wood and sailors into grinding holes; digging, with hideous booming slurps, its own mouth with its own food.

On they rolled, but more slowly now, with but one mast left, and that one cleaned of sails.

"The wyrld is steep," said Frduae, "but not steep enough. Feel the ship slowing, and we still have the bellsands to cross." She pointed with one bony finger at the Cities of the Well, nearer now, tiny lights flickering under their canopy of cloud. "We will never make it."

It was a slow slowing, but Kemen could feel it, sleeping after sleeping, in the lessened sound of the wheels. Rock and sand still sped by, but less hurriedly, and Kemen and Maer Ash looked at each other anxiously as the creaking of the ropes that held the ship together grew gradually louder than the rumble of the wheels that carried it.

They entered a range of low hills. The twisting path between them was dusted with traces of violet sand that rang under the wheels, distantly, like bells. It was a sound that caused the faces of the windsailors to knot in anxiety.

The ship was rolling no faster than a man could run when Kemen and Maer Ash saw on a ridgetop overlooking them what they had been looking for, and fearing, without knowing it: the first recognizable life they had seen since leaving the fleetpath and diving down the wyrld:

Hooded riders on ponies improbably tall.

SIX

PACED BY THE MENACING, HOODED figures that rode the ridgetops like light riding waves, the *Corec* passed through the last of the low hills. Below, at the bottom of a smooth plain, the Cities of the Well beckoned like a smoky jewel, near and yet impossibly far: for between the hills and the plain lay a narrow band of violet dunes that, according to Frduae, was impossible to cross without full sail. The bellsands.

The ship slowed sickeningly when the wheels hit the loud sand. Groaning, the helmsman spun the wheel and with shouts and screams the sailors turned the last sail; timbers cracking, the great ship turned and, losing speed more slowly, tacked along the edge of the bellsands, looking for a low place in the drifts.

On the deck, terror and confusion ruled. The sailors ran from side to side, rocking the *Corec* on its wheels as they looked in anguish first at

the bellsands that trapped them, then at the
eumen that stalked them. The robes of the
eumen flowed like water in the wind and only
their hands were visible, filled with curved
swords; only their eyes, deep in their hoods,
filled with cruel joy. They were silent, communi-
cating in a harsh radio whisper that Kemen
heard in the bone rather than the ear.

Mone appeared on deck, rubbing his eyes with
sticky hands. He separated Maer Ash from
Kemen and chained her to himself. He cowered
in his robes beneath one of the splintered masts,
eating nervously from a polished baby's skull,
while she paced around him in chain-length
circles.

The eumen were getting into formation; their
radio whisper was becoming a radio scream.

Kemen found a place at the war rail at the
bow, between a beaked Anthr with a poison
spear and a swordwoman of Coenti Jjl. The war
rail was crowded with specialized fighters from
many wyrlds, nervously blinking in the now
too-delicate wind, waiting to make their weapons ring like an orchestra of war. Each waiting
alone.

Kemen held the sword called Wyrldmaker at
his side, welcoming the numbness the stone
sent from his hand through his arm to his soul.
Even if it had been a trick, this is what he had
been taken aboard to do, and it was what he did
well. Killing.

The ship slowed to a fast walk. *Corec* would
have to try a crossing soon or it would be too late.
The eumen no longer dotted the ridgetops; they
flanked the ship in a crescent formation, a

hundred swords as bright as glass. The radio
waves of their war cry broke over the ship and
Kemen shivered in his robe.

Suddenly, the ship heeled and turned, taking
its chance, into the deep sands with a chorus of
bells; and just as suddenly stopped. The bellsands caught the *Corec* as a hand catches a ball,
ripping the last sail from the last mast, hurling
men and spars into the violet sand.

Just as suddenly, the eumen were upon them.

Kemen slashed down at the first of the hands
that appeared over the rail, and left six bone-
white fingers wriggling on the wood. More
hands, then heads, appeared: long of skull and
long of tooth, black eyes in white leathery skin,
long ribbony ears hidden deep in menacing
hoods, slit mouths parted in parting screams as
robed bodies fell among the ponies and severed
heads turned over and over in air.

War!

Cold as destiny in the hand was the sword
called Wyrldmaker. High was its killing song.
Sweet was its taste for bone and blood. Deep lay
the limbs at Kemen's feet as he danced the
dance called war.

He heard Maer Ash's triumphant scream and
turned to see her pulling a knife from the neck of
a eumen that was folding like a tent, as its spirit
moved out. Another eumen slashed at Mone,
then raised a sword from behind to split Maer
Ash's skull. Kemen leaped, crossing half the
deck in two long steps, and sliced off the legs
above the knee, so the eumen sat suddenly in a
slick pool of its own gore.

Mone was dying. He looked at Kemen pitifully,

clutching his wounded arm; it came away from his shoulder in his hand, and he held it like an instrument he had forgotten how to play. He lay back on the deck and stared at the light-streaked sky while his fine robes filled with blood.

"Are you all right?" Kemen asked Maer Ash. But she was already back in the fight, picking up the shattered swords from the deck and throwing them expertly into the cheeks and necks of the eumen clambering over the sides of the ship. Kemen slashed the chain that bound her to the dying Mone and ran back to the war rail at the bow.

His companions lay in pieces on the deck, all dead. The front of the ship was unguarded, but no more eumen were trying to come over the rail.

Kemen looked behind him and saw that the fight had shifted to the stern, and that it was done. The last windsailor to slash at the eumen who crowded over the rails paid for his boldness with a glass blade through his neck. The rest stood huddled in surrender: Frduae and eleven others.

Maer Ash was not among them.

The ponies ate flesh. The eumen dropped bodies and pieces of bodies over the sides of the ships to the violet sands. Then they tied the twelve captives in twos and bound them to the backs of six ponies, which were chewing noisily.

They ignored Kemen. He watched from the war rail, holding his sword, not knowing whether to attack or run. The eumen had clearly decided to avoid the Wyrldmaker by leaving Kemen alone. He was in no danger of being captured, yet he could see no chance of saving the others, against the sixty blades still left to the eumen.

He watched while they rode off into the hills, wondering what had happened to Maer Ash. He was alive but he had never felt so alone.

"Hey. You."

He looked down. Under the bow of the ruined ship, Maer Ash sat on a tall pony with three swords in her belt and her red hair matted with blood. She was grinning. Kemen climbed down and onto the pony behind her.

"I don't know your name," she said, "but come on."

Something was wrong. The pony was fast and smooth and strong. It carried them both easily, running tirelessly along the flat stones at the base of the hills. But it wouldn't go where they wanted; it wouldn't turn into the bellsands, no matter how Maer Ash kicked it and cursed it and tugged at its long black mane.

"Let it go," Kemen said. He took one arm from around Maer Ash and pointed down the wyrld, to the Cities of the Well. "We can walk. We can survive."

She shook her head. "Perhaps there's a way to ride. Maybe the sands give out. At least the pony will find water."

It did find water: a blue pool between two low hills. There was even a little grass, the first Kemen had ever seen. The pony drank, then knelt to let them off.

They rested. Kemen cleaned his blood-darkened sword on the sparse grass and Maer Ash washed her hair. They both laughed at how strange she looked with it plastered to her head. Kemen asked her how she had survived, and where she had learned war, for she had learned it somewhere well.

"I jumped, and hid under the ship when I saw that they were winning," she said. "I hid behind a wheel while the ponies ate the dead, and some that were not dead. I heard them ride off, and I found this pony left behind, as if it were waiting for me.

"I learned war young, for I am a mercie from beyond the mountains of Aer. We are masked women who fight for the highest bidder and are feared everywhere. I was on my way to Coenti Jjl to the Learnwyrlding when I was captured and enslaved by Mone.

"The Learnwyrlding? I do not know what it is, only that all mercies must learn it, for it concerns a treasure greater than all others in all the wyrlds, and we fight for treasure. And are we not good fighters? But come, our pony is rising and wants us to go. . . ."

It was like watching a tower build itself, and it took a long time. Manipulating its tree-long legs in a clumsy dance, the pony rose in stages, slipping, tripping, weaving its small body higher and higher into the air, lofting itself on its four-jointed limbs. At the last moment Kemen and Maer Ash caught the dangling mane and swung up.

The pony's legs were as thin as an oldling's wrist and twice as tall as a man; kneeling or standing, it looked clumsy, but running it was as graceful as wind in a woman's hair. Its eyes were not dull like those of most beasts but bright and mocking, and even as it ran it looked back at Kemen and Maer Ash knowingly.

"And where you lived, beyond the mountains of Aer," Kemen asked her, "did you ever hear of Llamp?"

"Never."

"For that is where I am bound."

The grass deepened and the hills grew higher as they rode, veering farther and farther from the violet dunes of the bellsands. Maer Ash clutched the pony's flying mane, and Kemen held her waist and told her of the love that had shattered his kingdom and brought him here. He told her of Noese, and Hayl, and the first time he saw fire. "I think love is like fire," he said. "Do you?"

She didn't answer. She seemed tired of talking. On they rode through the deepening grass. How quiet it was! For the first time since Kemen had left the smooth sea at the foot of the Wyrldwall, he heard no screams, no shouts, no clattering wheels or howling wind. There was just the soft rush of the pony's feet in the deepening grass as they turned back into the hills, and he laid his cheek across Maer Ash's back and slept.

He dreamed of his son, Hayl. He dreamed Hayl held Noese in the palm of his little hand, and she glowed like fire. She was naked.

He woke up and saw that they were on a high pass. The wyrld itself seemed a wall: far above were the gleaming mountains of Aer, and high on their slopes a single light that might have been Coenti Jjl; far below, a smoky mix of cloud and light, were the mysterious Cities of the Well. All around were soft hills clothed in long grass. Kemen wondered sleepily where the pony was taking them. He smiled and laid his hand on the sheath of the sword where it wasn't cold, and laid his cheek back down on Maer Ash's broad back under her rough robe and thought: I am no longer a stranger here. And went back to sleep.

When he awoke again the pony was kneeling and he was falling off.

He fell on top of Maer Ash, and by the time they had untangled themselves and stood up in the deep grass, the pony was loping off over a hill, looking back at them with one bright, mocking eye.

"It was a trick!" said Maer Ash.

Kemen looked around. Eight of the other captives, including Frduae, lounged in the grass nearby. They didn't even seem surprised, or even interested, to see Kemen and Maer Ash. Some slept, some nibbled on grass stems, some just stared up at the sky.

"Where are we?" Kemen demanded. "Are we captives?" He looked around for the eumen but they were nowhere in sight. No one answered him and he shook Frduae by the shoulder. "Don't you know me?"

"Of course," she said. She handed him a handful of long grass. "Have you eaten?"

"Not now," he said, waving her hand away. Frduae gave the grass to Maer Ash, who tried it. "It is food," she said. "It's not bad."

"It is food *and* drink," said Frduae, stuffing a

handful into her own old crack of a mouth. She grinned.

Impatient, Kemen left them and walked to the top of the hill, where the pony had disappeared. In a small valley below, a camp was built around three tall tents. He saw the eumen cleaning weapons and arranging loot in piles: daggers, belts, boots, boards. On a fire by the tents they were roasting two of the captives, one of them alive, while two others stood by yawning and watched impassively. The eumen worked tirelessly, purposefully, cleaning and arranging the camp, but they never spoke to one another. And where were the ponies?

As if in answer to Kemen's question, two ponies came out of the larger of the tents, examined the cooking meat, and after conferring briefly in a radio whisper that utterly chilled his bones, went back inside.

Kemen ran stumbling wildly back over the hill. "The eumen are the beasts!" he told Maer Ash. "It's the ponies that took the ship and captured us; the eumen are but their hands!"

"So?" She handed him a wad of grass and looked at Frduae and giggled.

"So! If we had only slain the ponies instead of fighting the eumen we might never have been captured." He ate hungrily while he talked. The grass was sweet but not filling. "If we don't escape now we will be eaten. They are eating two of us down there now."

"First we must eat," Maer Ash said. "We must rest." She took off her belt of swords, and rolled over in the grass, stretching and yawning.

Kemen shuddered, remembering the two captives who stood naked, watching the other two cook. He coughed and spat the grass into his hand and flung it away.

That was why there were no guards, no chains . . . the grass itself was their prison! He pulled Maer Ash to her feet and slapped her.

"We must go!" he shouted. "Maer Ash!"

She rubbed her red face and giggled. Frduae grabbed her arm and pulled her back down in the grass. Kemen kicked out with his heavy boot and heard the old woman's face bones snap.

"Now see what you did," Maer Ash chided. She took Frduae in her arms but found she was dead, and she laid her aside.

Kemen fell to his knees, his head spinning. He had killed her. They had to get out of here. He took off his sword and laid it aside so he could think. He pushed the sword called Wyrldmaker under a clump of grass where he would be sure to find it again. Perhaps if he asked her in a nice way. Walking was silly so he rolled through the grass until he found Maer Ash, laying in a pile with two others.

"What is it now?" she giggled.

He had forgotten.

SEVEN

KEMEN HAD NEVER SEEN A WYRLD up close before. As a boy he had seen the boats rising from the sea floor where they waited for the Lightening to float them; he had seen the blade, the net, the cutsjark's head on the cut-room floor. As a man his eye had filled with distance: Noese. Her very name to him meant far, and he had seen distance in her blue eyes even as their heads lay together that one time. He had seen distance, too, in the long look in a killed man's eye as his life recedes in a rush, and he had seen it in the blue stone. The killing stone. It had always been hard to hold it in the eye, so that looking into it was like looking far across the plain to the mountains of Aer, even when it was held in the hand.

But now he saw things up close. The shape of a finger, the cast of an eye, the delicate shadings of a blade of grass. Kemen was continually amazed to find that each part of the wyrld was as filled as the whole wyrld was with sounds and smells and things to see.

What good friends they all were! They'd done away with names as they'd done away with differences, and they spent their time agreeing in giggles on the fitness of things. There were still four of them left. There was plenty to eat. Kemen slept with his cheek in the curve of a green-eyed woman's back, with his now soft fingers caught in the tangles of a red-haired woman's hair. He slept.

He woke when they took her away.

They took two of them: her and a fat man who laughed a lot. They waved as they walked with the eumen to the top of the hill.

That left Kemen and one other. They ate together of the glisteny glistening grass, then Kemen rolled away to find water. He wasn't really thirsty but he was hungry for something and felt, curiously, unfilled. Perhaps it was water after all. They had always found it under the grass clumps where it was imprisoned in white roots just waiting for teeth to set it free. But even after he found water Kemen kept on looking until under one clump his hand touched something that made him pull his hand away, something as cold as the bark of death.

It was the sword called Wyrldmaker. Cold in his hand it filled him like food. Looking into the blue stone made his eyes howl and he looked away, then back, dazzled with distance. The wyrld itself seemed to pull back from him and he sat up and looked around, seeing the steep plain, the green hills, the overreaching mountains achingly far beyond, and nearby below the glittering smoky Cities of the Well.

"Maer Ash!" he cried.

The camp in the little valley was much changed from when he had seen it last. The piles of lumber, jewelry and trash were taller, indicating that there had been several more raids while he had slept and dreamed on the hillside. The fires were out, the tents were struck, and the ponies sat in the grass, talking and planning in low radio tones, while the eumen made the final preparations for another raid.

Kemen's knees and arms felt weak. Under his robe he clutched the hilt of the unsheathed sword, rejoicing in the killing pain it sent singing through his body. Pain sings. He stood at the top of the hill, scanning the camp for some sign of Maer Ash.

He was relieved to see that the cooking fires were out; but his relief turned to horror when he saw why. Maer Ash and the other were stretched out naked on a rock stained with blood, half-hidden behind one of the treasure piles of lumber. They were being prepared as cold food for the raid. The fat man's head had already rolled into the dust, and his limbs were being trimmed and fit into baskets lined with grass while Maer Ash yawned, sleepily awaiting her turn.

The eumen were too busy to notice the wild man in the filthy white robe running slantways down the hill through the deep grass, bearing a sword that flashed like a storm in a cloud; but the ponies saw him. Their radio whispers shivered the bones and the eumen looked around, then ran for their stacked blades.

They were fast. Before Kemen reached the bottom of the hill, four of them stood in his path, their curved blades uplifted like teeth. The others were gathered around the stone where Maer Ash lay, her neck extended and her wide eyes cloudy with dreams. Off to the side, in the deep grass, the ponies were beginning the long and complicated process of getting to their feet.

Kemen never slowed. Wyrldmaker sang and a eumen fell in two pieces like a rotten melon; another laid down its sword and held its hands at its belly like a basket to catch the warm, unfamiliar forms wriggling out of the seam that had been opened in its body. The two others were spit together in one thrust, then released to fall.

On he ran. The others waited, surrounding Maer Ash. Kemen was one and the eumen were many, and he would drown in the blood before he reached her, for none of them minded dying.

That was the ponies' plan, but Kemen fooled them. Just when the eumen blades were raised for the clash he cut suddenly sideways and dashed to deep grass at the side of the camp, where the ponies were working their way to their feet. His attack on the eumen had left them unprotected. Leaping, he caught the moon-colored mane of the largest pony, and swung up onto its neck just as it was lifting and locking its limbs.

Standing, the pony was transformed from an ungainly cripple to a thing as graceful as wind, and as arrogant; and the eye that regarded Kemen was bright with hate.

Kemen hooked his sword under the pony's neck, taking the hilt in one hand and the tip in the other, and pulled. The pony tossed its head, and Kemen pulled harder. "Call them off," Kemen said.

There was no sound but an ache in Kemen's bones. Four of the eumen grabbed Maer Ash and lay a blade against her throat. The rest gathered around the legs of the pony, looking up at Kemen with vacant stares.

Kemen pulled harder. "Call them off," he said. "Who fears the hand when the head is gone?" He gave the blade a little twist and blood began to ruin the pony's velvet coat.

His bones ached something else.

Surrender.

They rode and when they rode they rode like the wind. The grassy hills, the violet bellsands, the dull clattering rock of the plain: all flowed beneath the pony's hooves like water, but more swift. Kemen clung to the pony's neck, his sword still at its throat, and Maer Ash clung to Kemen's back, wrapped in the eumen's black and bloody robe.

"It was easy," Kemen boasted, "once their secret was discovered. Just as it is easy to make the pony cross the bellsands, cross the wyrld! For their secret is not their intelligence. It is the fear that thinking brings . . ."

Kemen pulled at the sword and the pony leaped on toward the Cities of the Well, fearing death!

Kemen talked on, but to himself. Maer Ash slept. She was still dazed and shaken, even though they had traveled several sleepings; how many, Kemen had no way of knowing, since he had not slept at all and Maer Ash had slept all the way.

The wyrld beneath them was a blur. The wyrld around them was as still and as splendid as the inside of a jewel. As they approached the bottom of the bowl-shaped plain, the mountains of Aer seemed even more impossibly high and distant. Kemen wondered how he was ever to reach them and cross them, to Llamp and Noese. Noese! The old twin fires of love and hope burned in his heart as he gazed at the lights in the near-distance; lights on the ground and lights in the clouds.

"The Cities of the Well," Maer Ash said. They were her first words since she had asked Kemen to eat the grass. At her suggestion they stopped on the plain outside the Cities of the Well and killed the pony. They carved off its head and carried it between them by the ears like a grimacing sack, to an inn where Maer Ash thought it might be traded for something better to eat.

EIGHT

WHAT SPLENDID CITIES THEY were to Kemen's eyes: three of them, built around, under, between, over and among one another in a spectacular jumble of ornament and ruin, disorder, grandness and noise.

The lights they had seen were fires, for the wooden city of Been was burning and being rebuilt constantly. At the center of Been, hidden behind a doorless porcelain wall, was star-shaped Wellkeaper, the sanctuary city where the well's invisible worshippers traded devotion for the metal that was the source of their trade. No one left or entered Wellkeaper, and the only signs of life from behind the walls were the screams that mingled with the mists boiling up from the roaring well. It was these mists, mixed with smoke, that formed the clouds Kemen had seen from the wyrld's rim.

Another city hung in the clouds overhead: Aer, named for the awesome peaks it hid from view.

From below it looked menacing, like a school of whales seen from the ocean floor. It was a city of stormwood towers, dark in the white mists, bobbing gently at the end of the long ropes that held them to the wyrld. It was here, it was said, that the wyzrd lived, and the merchants who traded in knives, and the warriors who wielded them.

And it was from Aer, Maer Ash said, that the airships left for Coenti Jjl.

"For Coenti Jjl!"

"Frduae was wrong," she said. "There is a way from here to Coenti Jjl, but not by windship. By air. I didn't tell you because I didn't think we would make it this far. Also because I hated you," she added with a smile, filling her wide mouth with thick sweet pony soup.

"Let us go then!" Kemen cried. "For Coenti Jjl is the way to Llamp, and Noese, and destiny."

"Let us eat first," said Maer Ash.

They were sitting in an inn in Been. The city was a maze of shacks, some of them ablaze, made from the debris of ships, built around Wellkeaper and extending in tall rickety towers high into Aer. It was here that the windsailors and the traders in wood and stormwood lived. The inn where they ate was called the Wooden Woman, because it was made entirely of the bow-decorations of hundreds of wrecked ships. In the wooden eyes of the wooden women were reflected all the horrors of the journey from the rim.

They had traded the pony's teeth to a jeweler, who had broken them from the jaw with the jaw of another pony and given Maer Ash a cloud-green cloak to replace her foul eumen robe; but the best they had been able to do with the head was give it to the inn-keeper who had thrown it into his soup in exchange for a place at his table.

So they dined on the being that would have dined on them, and Kemen wondered if he would have tasted quite so nasty.

After they had eaten, they walked through the smoky streets of Been, looking for a tower high enough to carry them to Aer. The streets were dark and narrow, deserted except for aged wind-sailors, their last voyages done, who stood talking softly in small groups, rubbing the stumps where their limbs had been and telling old lies.

A roaring filled the air, getting louder until the street dead-ended at a blank, porcelain, tooth-colored wall. The sight of it seemed to fill Maer Ash with terror, and she clutched Kemen's hand and hurried him off, down a side street and away from the roaring.

"That sound is the well," she said. "It is only heard and never seen, for no one enters Well-keeper."

"No one?"

"Only the dead. At the waterchanging great baskets filled with knives are passed out, over the wall. They are returned filled with these sailors who are waiting so patiently to die, who have traded their bodies for the food and drink of their last days."

Kemen looked at her sharply. "How do you know so much of the Cities of the Well," he asked, "who are from Coenti Jjl?"

"We mercies know many wyrlds," she said. "Look! There is the tower we seek."

The tower groaned with the weight of their steps. They could feel it swaying as they crossed from side to side, ascending the switchback stairs that were roped together out of odd-sized timbers and spars. The first, and longest, part of the journey was inside, and it was dark; the steps were half-lit with jars of glowing fluid tied to the leaning walls at long intervals.

Maer Ash went first. She was tireless. Kemen's thigh and knees ached, even though he felt lighter here than he had felt on the wyrld's rim. He longed to rest, but she plunged on as if she couldn't wait to leave the wyrld behind.

The endless stairs ended at a door, where an old man armed with a rusted knife demanded a toll.

"We have nothing!" Kemen said. They hadn't even kept one tooth from the pony's head.

"But we do!" Maer Ash. She caught the old man's leathery chin in her hand and stared at him. "Here's a treasure for you. Your life. We will leave your miserable head on its miserable neck, where it now sits, instead of twisting it off and rolling it down the stairs. Now stand aside." She kicked the door open and Kemen followed her through.

They were almost in the clouds. A ladder of boards and rope hung down from a stormwood tower, a dark shape looming in the mists overhead. As they climbed, Kemen remembered his death climb up the wyrldwall, only this time he looked back: he saw the tangled streets and burning roofs of Been, so far below it dizzied him; and in the center of them, the perfect five-pointed star of Wellkeeper; and in the center of that city the well itself, gaping like a mouth opened in a scream, filled with rushing white water.

"Look!" he said.

"Come on," she said, never pausing, and disappeared into the clouds.

Aer was a dream city, dim and quiet and empty. The streets were narrow paths of swaying boards, floating between great stormwood towers that spun slowly at the ends of ropes as thick as thin men. It was damp and dark inside the cloud; towers loomed out of the mist, then lingered like ghosts as they walked past, Kemen's boots sounding terrifyingly loud on the stormwood walks. It was a shadow city, with neither shape nor size, since all they ever saw was what was immediately beside, above or below them. They walked and walked and never saw a soul.

Kemen was looking for the wyzrd.

Maer Ash was looking for the oldest tower in Aer.

That would be their airship, Maer Ash explained. "Old towers are traded for new," she said, "just as it is with the ships that sail the rim. When enough stormwood is gathered to build a new tower, the oldest one in Aer is filled with knives and cut loose. It drifts with the clouds and shatters on the slopes of the mountains of Aer, not far from Coenti Jjl. That tower is the tower we must find. Forget this wyzrd."

"How often does this happen?" Kemen asked.

"Once in a lifetime when a lifetime is short," she said. "Twice, I hope, if one is luckier than any being has the luck to be."

They were lucky.

Even through the mist the new tower gleamed: fresh yellow paint on freshcut stormwood boards. The massive doors were not yet hung, and they walked through the empty rooms, shouting, until the answers of their own echoes convinced them that there was no one there.

"It's almost finished!" Maer Ash said. Kemen had never seen her look so giddy. She spun around on her heel and then did something she had never done before: stretched upward on her tiptoes and kissed his big, scarred cheek.

She caught his hand and they ran out, hurrying across the narrow walkways, finding it easy not to fear a fall they couldn't see, and found the old tower only three towers away.

Its narrow windows blazed with lights. Its wide porch was rotted, and the railing was hanging and broken. The door was old, the steps were old, the old halls were filled with musty smells. Dust and shadows and stacks of knives filled the lower rooms. As they raced up the stained and broken stairs they could hear voices and laughter from above. Kemen and Maer Ash stopped, out of breath, and grinned at each other before pushing open the last sagging door.

Inside it was warm and steamy. There was a fire and the smell of food, and a long table filled with Moidor and winged Poplei and people and other beings, eating and drinking happily, preparing for a long journey.

But something was wrong.

The room fell quiet as Kemen pushed the door shut behind them. Maer Ash gasped, gathering breath for a scream that was never to come.

At the head of the table sat Mone.

"Thief," he said, smiling at Kemen.

Kemen's arms were suddenly pinned behind his back and he turned his head and saw a grinning, slot-marked face.

Misk.

NINE

K EMEN AWOKE IN A DUNGEON OF
sky.

His sword was gone. His robe was gone. He
was chained by one ankle to a ring in the center
of a small stormwood raft floating above the
clouds. He was naked. He was alone.

He put his hand to the back of his head where
it ached and brought it back wet with his own
unfamiliar blood. He remembered darkness
first: then violence, shouts, betrayals, as the
memory of what happened opened in his mind
like the door to a room he did not want to
enter. . . . He had shouted: "Run!"

But Maer Ash didn't run.

The room fell as still as a dead man's heart
and she looked from Mone to Misk to Kemen
with her wide eyes narrowed and did something
that caused Kemen's heart, even now, remembering, to break its long stride.

Stepping back to Kemen's side, she shouted to

Mone: "Watch him, he's armed!" She reached beneath Kemen's robe and ripped loose the sword called Wyrldmaker, still in its sheath, and threw it clattering across the floor. It slid under the table where Mone sat. Gathering her own robes around her like a queen, Maer Ash followed the sword and sat at the table beside Mone.

Kemen was speechless. Maer Ash was looking down at her clasped hands when Misk smashed him across the back of the head with an iron goblet decorated with scenes of a half-eaten banquet. . . .

It was cold on the raft and Kemen's head ached like a blood bell.

Betrayed.

He stood up; the raft tipped sickeningly, and he dropped back to his knees. He lay on his stomach and peered over the edge. The raft bobbed at the end of a long rope that descended into the clouds below. In the swirling mists he could see suggestions of shapes: the half-hidden towers of Aer. Beyond the clouds on every side the awesome plain rose to the wyrld's rim; and on one far side of that rim rose the still-distant mountains of Aer. Single clouds, like sheep, formed a long line from the cloudbank to the mountains' lower slopes.

Above, neither nearer nor farther than it had ever been, was the familiar dull-gray sky, scratched with long streaks of light.

Betrayed.

The chain was longer than the raft; long enough so that if Kemen fell he would hang by one ankle, upside-down, staring into the clouds not far below. There was no food or water on the raft. He was cold.

Betrayed by the one friend he'd found in two wyrlds—for even in his own lost sea wyrld rimmed with wall he'd traveled and fought alone. Betrayed. He remembered waking from his dream on the *Corec* and showing Maer Ash the secret of the Wyrldmaker, and he marveled at his own foolishness. He had betrayed himself. So be it. He had left to him now only the cold blue distant memory of Noese; no Hayl, no sword, no blue stone and, as far as his eye could see, no chance of escape from his prison in the sky. He was impatient to die once again.

He slept, and when he woke a yellow bird with one eye and one leg was perched on the ring at the center of the raft. It stared at him patiently until he wrung its neck and ate it raw, licking the blood from his hands carefully.

He slept. He woke. He was in a dead, still wyrld without wind or sound; the only movement was the gentle movement of the raft as it drifted at the end of its rope. At long intervals, the birds arrived; his eat and drink. It was like eating the same one over and over. He slept. He woke. Once he heard a rising sound like a cheer from below, and he looked down to see a tower rising from the clouds, spinning grandly. Blazing with lighted jars, it was the oldest tower he and Maer Ash had found, the one where Mone had captured him. It rose, its rope dangling, half-in and half-out of the mists; it drifted toward the edge of the cloudbank, while tiny figures on the rotten porches waved at the mists below. No one looked up at him. He couldn't pick out Maer Ash, or Misk, or Mone.

Betrayed. Alone. So be it. Still, for the first time since he'd sat on Hayl's empty bed, he felt like weeping as he watched the tower break from the cloudbank, drift into the line of single clouds stretching toward the mountains of Aer, and begin the long process of getting smaller and smaller.

He slept. He woke. Once, the bird brought an extra meal: the grinning cooked head of a half-man-sized creature with cracked skin like a well-worn glove and dark little eyes like raisins. Kemen ate the bird and nibbled at the head. The eyes tasted like things that had been left too long in the sea. He made the head last through three more birds.

Kemen slept and his sleep was empty of dreams.

He woke startled. The raft was descending in long, smooth steps toward the clouds. Already the first cold fingers of mist were reaching around the edges, and Kemen shivered as the cloudbank swallowed him. The plain, the awesome mountains, the wyrld's high rim all disappeared in the gray half-darkness. He leaned over the edge and saw a shape looming nearer in the mists below. It was the new tower they had found, now finished and painted gold and green. On the top-most balcony, pulling in the rope with easy motions like a fisher who fishes the sky, grinning, was Misk.

He tied the raft level with the balcony and

motioned to Kemen with a two-bladed sword.
Kemen stepped off, deciding to see for himself
what new horrors life had to offer; the chain
pulled him up short and Misk unlocked it at his
ankle with a slot in the point of the sword.

Draped over the railing was Kemen's own
travel-stained robe: the once-white dying robe
he had taken from the great hall at pasTreyn,
now red with dust and blood. He slipped it on.
Misk was holding a wire with a loop in one end
and a handle in the other. He put the loop
around Kemen's little finger and pulled it tight.
Then, still without a word, he turned and walked
through the jar-shaped doorway.

Kemen hesitated until the wire jerked a bright
ring of blood around his finger, then followed.

At the end of the long hall that smelled like
new wood, Misk released Kemen's finger and
pushed him through a doorway. Kemen heard
the door close behind him. He was alone in the
room with Mone.

He had watched him die on the deck of the
Corec, when the deck was awash with blood.
Now he saw him sit on a massive pile of pillows
in a room lighted with bowls of glowing fish,
chewing and scratching the blueish flesh of his
new arm with the pink, ring-heavy fingers of his
old one. The new arm grew out of his shoulder
where the other had been sliced off by the blades
of the eumen. It was almost full-sized, though
the fingers had not yet separated enough for
rings. They looked obscenely naked.

"What do you want with me?"

"Treasure," Mone said. "Revenge. Assistance.
Sit. Eat."

He pushed a tray toward Kemen; it was filled with insects trying unsuccessfully to escape from the sweet syrup that covered them.

Kemen was hungry and he ate greedily. He had given up hope in his prison in the sky, and with it fear, and when he spoke he spoke boldly.

"You have lied to me," he said. "You have betrayed me, stolen from me, attacked and imprisoned me. Now, whether you mean to threaten, cajole, reward or kill me, it is all the same. I have nothing to say to you."

Mone looked hurt. "You are right to mistrust me," he admitted. "I am a low creature. I lied even when I confessed that I had lied, for I said that lying was my most grievous fault. It is not. Greed is. All that I do I do for gain. For treasure . . ."

Leaning toward Kemen, he looked like a stack of robes and rings about to fall over. His old hand reached into the bowl and fed his wide mouth, then went back to scratching the new arm.

"It is of treasure that I wish to speak," he said. "First, the woman. Maer Ash . . ."

Kemen tried to look disinterested. "First you speak of treasure, then of slaves," he said scornfully.

"She is no slave! She was my captive, but that was only because of her high station. She is the Bride of the Dead. To her is given the task of accompanying the corpses to the wyrld's center, where souls are traded for knives. It is a great honor and she is a greater fool. She somehow learned war and escaped Wellkeeper, and it was my task to bring her back. My reward is this magnificent tower in which we sit. Do you like it?"

"So you have it," Kemen spat. "What is it you want with me?"

"More treasure. I have discovered, quite by accident, that there is an even greater bounty on you." Mone smiled. Even if he had had teeth it would not have been a pleasant smile. "More precisely, on the sword you bear. Is it not called Wyrldmaker?"

"Certainly not," Kemen lied. He sickened and remembered the wyzrd's warning. He thought he had given up all his hopes of reaching Noese, but he found he hadn't: he could feel them fleeing now. Then they just as suddenly returned, for Mone reached behind his mountain of pillows and pulled forth the familiar long sword in its short scabbard. It looked dull and lifeless in his fat hands. The blue stone was gone!

"You lie so poorly," Mone said. "Here is a treasure even greater than you know, greater than all the treasures of all the wyrlds."

"Whatever it is," Kemen said cautiously, "you have it now."

Mone shook his head: first the nose shook, then the plump cheeks, then the chins as countless as rings. "No, I don't. The stone that gives it life is gone. I myself didn't notice, until I took it to the wyzrd in Aer to gloat, for the wyzrd also seeks the treasure that is the sword, and I wanted him to know he was beaten."

Kemen tried to keep his face from betraying the pounding of his heart. The wyzrd must have taken the stone! What a fool he had been not to go to the wyzrd first; the wyzrds were his allies in the search for Noese, and he should never have listened to Maer Ash and sought the tower first. She had betrayed him in more ways than one.

"Where is this wyzrd now?" he asked, casually, he hoped. "What did this wyzrd say?"

Mone hid the sword back behind the pile of pillows. "What he said was nothing. What he did was laugh at me until the windows of his mean little tower shook. Where he is now is on the barge with the dead awaiting their Bride; the bigger portion of him, that is. The bottom part.

"His head you ate."

Kemen felt as if he had fallen from a great height, and just hit bottom. He stared blankly at Mone; hope, fear, even hatred was gone.

"I will trade you your life for the blue stone," Mone said.

It was Kemen's turn to laugh, and his own laughter was the cruelest sound he'd ever heard. It was a barking sound. "After all this, after all the horrors in all the wyrlds, do you think it is death I fear?" he scoffed. He wasn't going to give Mone the satisfaction of knowing that he didn't know where the stone was. It didn't matter anyway. Without it, there was nothing to live for: no sword, no mission, no Llamp, no Noese.

"To put it another way," Mone explained, "I will have the stone or watch you die."

"Death. It has a sweet sound to me," Kemen said. It was true. He had started this journey seeking death, and now he was anxious to complete it.

Mone filled his mouth with furry grapes and passed another bowl to Kemen. "I was afraid you would feel that way," he said. "And in fact you have caught me in yet another lie. Death you must have anyway, for your passage has already been booked on the barge. The priests who rule Wellkeeper insist on it, for they want back the treasure you stole from them. They want you for the ceremony, and then for the voyage, but I have struck a bargain with them for the time between. For the ceremony, they need a living man. For the voyage, a pail of meat will serve, as long as it is you."

Mone rapped on the floor and Misk entered the room, prodding Kemen with his two-pointed sword and his pierced grin. He wrapped Kemen's hands in a chain behind his back, while Mone took out the sword and pulled it from its sheath. Without the stone it was no longer than its sheath, but the edge glistened keenly as Mone tested it with his new, nail-less thumb.

"After the ceremony," he said, "I will cut you into pieces myself with your own sword. Very small ones, very slowly. You and I will feast together on your flesh until you are ready to trade for death what you would not trade for life. Then I will have the stone."

Kemen stared at him as he was being pushed out the door:

"What ceremony? What treasure I stole from them?"

"You are learning to lie better. It's a pity you have no life left to use your new skill. The ceremony is the wedding. The treasure, of course, is the jewel that gives value to the Bride of the Dead, just as the stone gives life to the sword.

"Her virginity."

TEN

WELLKEEPER LAY FAR BELOW AND straight below. Misk led Kemen, chained, down the halls and stairs of Mone's new tower; down a shaky spiral walk that hung from the new-cut porches; down to the top of a porcelain tower that connected clouds and wyrld. With the one hilt of his two blades Misk rapped on the door and delivered Kemen to the four masked warriors who opened it. They shut the door behind them, leaving Misk to wait in the swirling clouds.

These are the mercies, Kemen thought, *if anything Maer Ash told me was true.* Two went in front of him and two behind. They were tall women with broad, scarred arms, clothed in chitin armor. Their faces were covered with featureless masks and the backs of their heads were bald. They carried no swords. Each was hung with a rack of winged knives.

They descended a long stairs, winding around

the inside of the tower. The steps and the walls glowed dimly, as if the porcelain itself were made partly of light. No one spoke. Everything here was clean and cold.

How could it be? Kemen wondered. Her virginity? Not when they had been captives of the ponies in the grassy hills; that had been all softness, not the hard piercing lightlike joy he had known with Noese and imagined love to be. He remembered waking on the deck of the *Corec* with his hand pocketed between her breasts; but that had been a dream of Noese. After his dream he had shown her his sword, but that was not the same as love.

And she had used it to betray him! He wondered if he would see her again, and hoped he wouldn't and wished he would.

The roar of the waters got louder as they descended until the air seemed thick with it. They passed several windows but Kemen could see nothing through them but swirling mists. It was as light inside the tower as outside.

The stairs ended in a pointed arch. They walked outside, onto a long parapet. It reached from the tower to a hall of white porcelain, with no windows or ornaments of any kind. Now Kemen could see the well below. It was a gash in the wyrld, filled with white water; it was long and narrow, about the size of the deck of the *Corec*. It looked to Kemen like a ship made of water in a sea made of wyrld.

The two sides and one end of the well were rough stone; the other end was a stairway that led down from the porcelain hall toward which they were walking. Anchored to these steps with a single rope, an elaborately carved barge was being loaded with corpses. As Kemen and his guards passed and entered the hall, he saw that the corpses were being carried by red robed men and stacked on the barge as carefully as if they were glass.

Inside the hall was one huge room, neither light nor dark but filled with the cold glow of porcelain. At one end the dead waited in piles to be carried down the stairs to the barge. At the other, in front of a bone white altar, stood an old man in a red robe with lizard skin and lidless eyes. And with him stood Maer Ash.

The mercies unchained Kemen and waited by the door while he walked across to her. She said nothing and Kemen said nothing. Only the water spoke in an endless musical shout. Her green eyes looked blank.

Her skin glowed golden, her red hair was cut short and carefully combed, and she was dressed all in white. A long gown covered her arms, her shoulders, even her neck and her feet. Only her face and her breasts were bare.

"So this is he," the man said, "who would take what belongs to the dead. But the law remains. The Waterchanging is almost here. The journey begins, and you must sanctify in death what you desecrated in life. Death is not cheated. You two are to wed."

He spoke in a whisper that sounded like ponies at war, and Kemen hardly listened. He searched Maer Ash's eyes with a thousand questions, and got not one answer. She met his eyes with a faraway green, almost-laughing look. Her cheeks and her nipples were rouged and she was, he realized with some surprise, beautiful.

The old man was still talking as he led them to the altar. "Do not speak. Touch but once. Wed and you will embrace in death, for who will replenish the waters if not we with our tears. . . ."

The old man joined their hands. Maer Ash's was not cold but warm. Kemen tested it but she didn't squeeze back. Still chanting, the old man pulled a lighted wand filled with desperate glowing creatures from his robe and waved it over their heads. He touched Maer Ash's head, and then her lips; then Kemen's head and lips. He indicated they were to kiss.

To Kemen's surprise, they kissed like lovers kiss, long and deep, and then Maer Ash was gone, hurried away by the old man. Kemen was hurried away by the four mercies who crossed the hall to chain his arms again. Kemen smiled at them. He smiled as they led him across the parapet and up the stairs of the tower. He smiled at Misk as they ascended into Aer, where he was to be sliced into pieces, small ones and slowly, which he would then have to eat. He smiled because he understood now why Maer Ash had taken his sword. His smile was as distant as hers; as cold as the cold of her kiss; as grim and as blue as the stone that lay in the back of his mouth where her tongue had pushed it. The blue stone.

Misk rapped on Mone's door. Kemen stood behind him. He knew that if he could get the stone into his hand, he would be armed with the

Wyrldmaker and free, but his hands were still chained behind his back. Mone grunted from within. Misk reached for the handle of the door, and Kemen stepped back. He had to make his move now, while the warrior's broad back was turned, even though he had no plan but to trust in the luck, and the stone, that had brought him this far.

He brought his knee up hard between Misk's legs.

Misk bellowed with rage and pain. Hurt but not slowed, he turned and lunged, pinning Kemen's neck to the wall between the twin blades of his sword. Kemen froze; the space between the blades was narrow, and even without moving he felt the steel slicing into his neck on both sides, the warm blood trickling down onto his shoulders.

Misk howled in triumph and hammered his fist into Kemen's stomach. Kemen coughed, spat, and the stone arched through the air and into the warrior's open mouth.

Misk's great greenish teeth snapped shut and he backed away, surprised, pulling his sword with him. He raised it over his head and advanced on Kemen again, more slowly this time. His smile widened and looked even more vicious as the cracks between his teeth grew red. His eyes drew back into his heavy, wolf-like head. He opened his mouth as if to scream and blood gushed out, painting his beard.

He dropped his sword and reached into his mouth, his fingers closing over the hilt of the sword called Wyrldmaker at the back of his throat. He pulled it out of himself, as if he were a sheath. It was half again as long as half a man and wet with gore. Misk swayed and fell and the sword fell beside him.

Kemen leaned over, and the sword cut through his chains as easily as if they were flesh. He took it up in both hands and kicked open Mone's door.

Mone was humming a soft song. He looked up, surprised. He sat on the pile of pillows fondling a naked creature that lay in his arms. It had one pink arm that ended in fingers heavy with rings, and the rest of its body was blueish and smooth. Its unformed face was Mone's. The arm he had lost on the *Corec* had grown a new body, just as the body had grown a new arm.

Kemen was startled, but only for a moment. The coldness of the sword in his hands propelled him forward, even before he understood what he was seeing.

Two Mones to kill!

The Mones panicked. Reaching behind the pillow, they found the sheath but the sword was gone. It was in Kemen's hand, singing like a choir of killers. Kemen took off both Mones' heads with one cut, then sliced methodically with a familiar, cold skill until the room was thick with the stench of life that has become meat only.

He strapped on the sheath and ran from the room, but he didn't sheath the sword. He thrilled to the cold, murderous feeling it gave his hand, and the hope it gave his heart. To Llamp! To Noese! He was bearing the Wyrldmaker again!

But first he had a score to settle. He would release Maer Ash just as she had released him.

He leaped over Misk's body and ran down the stairs of the tower; he jumped the broad porches and hit the planks that led down to Wellkeaper. Here he paused for only an instant. Behind him was the manthick rope that bound Mone's tower to the wyrld. He cut it with one slash of the sword. The tower began to spin slowly and drift away as he ran down the planks toward the porcelain entrance to Wellkeaper.

Two mercies opened the door. One closed it with her falling body, disemboweled by a blade as swift as wind is hard to see. The other fell backward and her tumbling corpse accompanied Kemen halfway down the stairs before wedging on a landing. Something was changed. Kemen didn't realize what it was until he reached the first of the narrow windows and looked out. The mist was gone. The roar of the water was gone. Wellkeaper was loud with a strange and terrifying silence.

He stopped at the next window and saw that the water in the well below was still. The barge was filled with corpses, and Maer Ash was being led down the steps toward it by red-robed men with lizard eyes. Kemen ran on.

The parapet was guarded by mercies who stood in twos at intervals along the wall. Their eyes were on the ceremony in the well below and they had no time to draw their knives as Kemen gathered their heads with his blade as greedily as a child strips berries from a branch. He left the parapet behind him rolling with heads and leaped over the wall and onto the steps.

The water was no longer still. It was dancing,

flecked with white, and the roar was rising. Maer Ash was chained to a post in the bow of the barge, which shook on the water and strained at the rope that held it. One of the lizard-eyed men was leaning over Maer Ash's exposed breast with a sawtoothed knife, while the other held a cleaver poised over the rope. Both were speaking in unison in a deep ritual chant: "So now, at the water-changing, let the wyrld, accept our thankful, dead . . ."

A winged knife flashed across Kemen's eyes. Another bit his ear. Two mercies sprang up on the steps before him, reaching into their racks for another throw, but too late: one he spit on his blade through the throat, the other he split lengthwise; she was white inside, slowly turning pink, then red, as she fell in two directions at once. Kemen leaped to the back of the barge.

A hundred empty eyes looked up at him as he scrambled over the stacked corpses. The only sounds were the hoarse panting of his breath, the rising roar of the water, and the singing of the sword called Wyrldmaker. The being that bent over Maer Ash stood up, startled, its eyes crossed, trying to focus on the steel that had passed between them. Kemen kicked the body over the side and struck at the other.

The sword sang as it tasted neck, but as the head spun off over the water it was grinning in triumph, for the headless body on the deck was finishing the task it had begun: in a last and mindless act the arms brought the cleaver down and split the rope.

The corpse tumbled over the side as the barge

began to spin free on the current. The roar of the water grew louder as the barge plunged toward the black hole at the other end of the well.

Kemen turned to Maer Ash. She was sobbing. "Fool," she said. "Why are you here? Now we are both dead!"

ELEVEN

IT WAS DARK UNDER THE WYRLD. Black water, black air, huge black booming sounds as the barge hit the walls of the cavern and spun off, then hit again, then rushed on; then only the black rushing roar of the water carrying them down.

With his hands Kemen found Maer Ash. He cut the chains that bound her to the pole and sat beside her in the bow. The only light was the blue stone in the hilt of the sword and Kemen laid it across his knees and looked into it. It lighted only itself and seemed, as always, far away.

"Fool," Maer Ash said again.

Kemen said nothing. He had hoped to free her and then be on his way to Llamp, and Noese, but here he was: bearing the sword he was born to bear but bearing it into a black and endless hole. The joy he had felt was gone. So was the fear. All he felt was foolish.

The cavern through which they rushed was narrow and twisting; black mud rained down on them as the barge boomed off the black walls. Maer Ash's voice in the darkness beside Kemen was dark with anger.

"Why do you fight?" she said. "For the joy of swinging your long sword? You saved me for what you see here, and you see nothing."

Kemen said nothing.

"You cheated a priest out of a meal but you didn't cheat death, for this is death! You cut the chain but it was not the chain that bound me to this voyage, for here I am! Did you think I wanted your company?"

"Do you think I want to listen to your complaints?" Kemen said, angry himself. "You complain if you live and complain if you die. Why are you angry with me?"

"Because you were the one thing I saw shining in all the wyrlds. You had a mission, you even told me of it. And now you have abandoned it."

"For you . . ."

"For the joy of swinging your sword," she said again. "This is not your destiny. It is mine, and I was a fool for trying to escape it, just as you are a fool for leaping into it."

"Then you lied to me."

"Of course I lied to you. Who in all the wyrlds has not lied to you?"

On they rushed into nothingness. Kemen felt her shiver in her thin wedding robe and he wrapped his robe around them both. Her rich smell mingled with the smell of the dead and the mud and he remembered, suddenly, the treasure he was accused of stealing.

"Maer Ash . . ." he began.

"Oh that," she said, as if she could read his mind. "That was my foolishness. I thought that by cheating death of my virginity I could cheat death of my life."

"But it never happened!" Kemen protested. "The charge was false."

"It happened. I made it happen. Remember the dream before you showed me the secret of the sword called Wyrldmaker? How sweet was that dream?"

Kemen felt his face flush in the darkness as they rushed on into the wyrld. He didn't remember the dream in detail but he remembered that it had been very sweet.

It grew colder but it could grow no darker. As they plunged on into the wyrld their limbs grew gradually heavier, and the shout of the water seemed to drop as if the wyrld itself were slowing down from its own weight. They slept.

While Kemen cut up a stiffened corpse for food, Maer Ash pulled a robe from a Noeri to cover herself against the deepening chill. Together, in the dark, they rearranged the stacked bodies and built themselves a shelter against the cold with walls of dead.

"Eat," said Kemen. The flesh was foul. They ate. They forgot what it was to see. Their limbs grew heavier until it was an effort to lift the strips of skin to their mouths. Side by side, they sat and talked until they could read each other's voices like faces.

"I learned war from the mercies," Maer Ash said. "About that I didn't lie. Each of the Virgins of the Well has a keeper from the high slopes of the Mountains of Aer. Mercies are masked and not supposed to love, but mine loved me. She taught me the secrets of the knives that fly and told me of Coenti Jjl and the Learnwyrlding. She taught me how to kill and died smiling with two knives she had given me sheathed in the little hollow at the base of her throat. Her name was Son and I never saw her face."

"Then you really were trying to get to Coenti Jjl."

"About that I was not lying. About that and the Learnwyrlding."

"This Learnwyrlding," Kemen said. "What is it?"

"It is said to contain the secret of life in the wyrlds, but that I do not know. I do not think there is a secret of life. I only know that searching for it gave meaning to my life for a while. One must seek something."

"I learned war from the sword," Kemen said. "And love from the boy it gave me." He told Maer Ash about Hayl and his little hands and little swords. They sat with the sword on Kemen's lap. The blue stone glowed but it gave no light; even when they held their hands together next to it their fingers were invisible in the darkness. Like something far away, the blue stone lighted only itself.

On they rushed. Deeper. Colder. Heavier.

They slept and when they woke they couldn't move.

The barge was not moving. The water was

still. There was no sound. Kemen's fingers each weighed as much as a city, each arm as much as a wyrld. He felt as if he were being pressed into the deck. He strained to fill his lungs with air against the weight of the wyrld; he dragged his fingers across the deck and found Maer Ash's hand.

He could hear her straining to breathe. Then she spoke, lifting the words like great stones.

"This. Then. Is. Death."

Kemen rested, then answered.

"No. Listen."

A low gurgling sound was coming toward them. As it grew louder they heard a wet clacking, like loose ribs. There was a moist, foul snort; a *thunk* near them as something hit the front of the barge; a sharp jerking motion . . . and the barge began to move, following the gurgling, clacking sound.

They were being towed.

First came the smell, then the light. At the beginning it was just a faint, unfamiliar odor mixed with the familiar smell of death and musk and sweat and clotted blood. But gradually it filled the air until it was the air itself: a sharp, painful stink of ancient rot and foul plants and fouler beings; crisp and acid and as loud in the senses as a scream. It enveloped Kemen and Maer Ash like smoke, curling their lips and making their guts heave until their every laborious breath was an agony.

The light came more slowly, but the vision it brought was as foul as the smell of the air. First the black softened to a doomy gray, then faded to a flat bone ash: the color of a wyrld without color.

Struggling against the weight that pressed them down, Kemen and Maer Ash sat up and saw that they were being towed across a still sea, through a vast cavern, toward a hideous island, by a giant insect with six clacking, oarlike legs. On its back two faceless beings with their muscles outside their skin like ropes fed whole corpses head first into a grinding hole in the center of the beast's back. The hole snorted gray, stinking smoke.

"Death. Is. Not. This. Foul." Maer Ash said.

The island ahead was of ore and stone. It was lighted by glowing, dripping fronds that hung down from the ceiling of the cavern; like pleading arms they weaved and waved, reaching for and feeding on the stinking smoke that belched upward from the backs of the giant insects that swarmed over the island.

Two barges were beached on the shore. One was being loaded by the faceless, rope-skinned beings with ore and dirt and the droppings of a great insect that was chewing noisily against the side of a blunt hill. Another was already stacked high with chain and knives and bars of iron and gold.

Kemen and Maer Ash stood between the legs of the stacked dead, straining to hold themselves up against the weight that was pulling them down. As they approached the island the insect that was pulling them let go with its long, hooked tail and scrambled up the beach, leaving them to drift slowly in.

Four of the corded beings waited for the barge. Even their heads were wrapped with muscle, and from their tiny mouths whip-long tongues swept the beach in restless movements. They spoke in whistles from holes where their noses might have been.

The sword called Wyrldmaker was sheathed under Kemen's robe, but its light glowed through; it was the only color in this underwyrld wyrld, and it seemed to him that it announced their presence like a shout. Holding to the stiffened ankle of a dead man he began to position himself so he could cover it, or draw it, when Maer Ash's words stopped him.

"They. Don't. See. Us. They. Have. No. Eyes."

With a jolt, the barge stopped in the shallow water and the corded beings climbed aboard.

Summoning all his strength, Kemen pulled Maer Ash to the side of the barge farthest from the shore. He helped her over the side and into the cold, shallow water, then followed her. With her hands on his back she tried to ease him down, but the weight was too much and they both fell down in the water. It jarred their bones and made a loud splash, but the beings on the barge unloading the dead didn't even look down.

"Nor. Ears." Kemen said.

They started for the shore. The water came to their waists. It was bitter cold but it buoyed them up and made it barely possible to walk. Kemen felt as if he were carrying himself and four others on his shoulders.

Kemen stopped, and stopped Maer Ash with a touch. There was nowhere to go. If they went up onto the beach, they would not be able to walk without the water to hold them up. Even in the water they would soon grow exhausted and fall, and not be able to get up again.

Suddenly, behind them from the barge, they heard whistles. Kemen looked back and saw the corded things clustering excitedly at the front of the boat around the pole where Maer Ash had been bound. Their long tongues played up and down the pole, lingering on the cut chains. They missed their bride.

More whistles, and louder ones came from the beach, from the blunt, stinking hills, from the clacking backs of the smoking insects. From every direction faceless, corded things ran toward the barge, their tongues making gray-wet circles in the air in front of them.

Kemen tried to draw the sword but it was far too heavy. Maer Ash stumbled back, into his arms. They watched, fascinated and terrified, as the beings consulted in whistles then fanned out to search the beach and the water with their flickering tongues.

The great insects continued their smoking and stinking and chewing, swarming across the dim hills and in and out of the water as if nothing were happening. Down the beach, near the other barges, one of them plunged into the water. Two of the rope-skinned things on its back fed corpses into its ceaselessly grinding maw, unconcerned with the search the others were carrying on.

Straining, Maer Ash lifted her arm and pointed.

"Look. Leave. Ing."

The insect was groping with its tail for the ore-filled barge beached on the shore ahead of them. Kemen and Maer Ash stumbled toward it through the water. Wherever it was being taken, it was their only chance.

Two of the corded things searched the shore between Kemen and Maer Ash and the barge. Their tongues flickered across the broken bones and shattered ore of the beach, then out across the gray water. The tongues seemed endless: six times as long as a man could reach. The first time one went between Kemen and Maer Ash they froze in terror, then plunged on. They were almost to the barge. It was starting to move . . .

Then something touched Kemen's face. The thing on the beach whistled excitedly, then flicked its tongue across Kemen's arms, his back, his neck, his head, discovering his shape and size. The touch was cold and foul, and Kemen's terror was complete.

Maer Ash had one hand on the barge when she heard his scream.

The tongue was as strong as a rope of iron. It wrapped itself around Kemen's neck and chest, pinning one arm to his side and pulling him toward the beach. The faceless things were fast. Five leaped off the barge of the dead and were running toward them through the water. Others were running across the beach. The stinking air was filled with excited whistles.

"The. Sword." Kemen groaned.

He tried to pull it from its sheath but it was far too heavy. It slipped from his hand and fell back with a loud ring. It was like trying to lift a ship out of the water.

Then he felt Maer Ash's hands on the hilt beside his own. Together, they strained, their feet slipping under them. Kemen's face went under the stinking water . . . but the sword came free!

In his hands it was light. He slashed the tongue that held him and the corded thing pulled the stump back with a wet *slup*, then a whistled scream. Kemen slashed two more that reached for him. The water was filled with faceless whistling things.

"Don't. Fight. Flee." Maer Ash was pulling at his arm. The barge was grinding across the bones, then floating free. Kemen grabbed the side as the barge pulled away and left the faceless things behind, whistling in confusion, searching with their useless hands for their severed tongues.

Maer Ash was on the barge. Kemen pulled himself up and dropped over the side and lay beside her on the sharp-edged ore. The whistling fell behind until the only sound was the clattering of insect legs and the chomping of insect maw.

The last thing Kemen saw before his eyes closed in exhaustion were the foul smokefronds on the roof of the cavern, reaching down for the stinking smoke, waving as if saying farewell.

TWELVE

KEMEN LIFTED HIS HEAD FROM Maer Ash's lap. Easily. He lifted a finger, then an arm. It felt light! He sprang to his feet, feeling as strong as a bird or a bird-boned boy. He grinned at Noese but she was still sleeping, wrapped in the blood-darkened robe of a dead Noeri, cradled in the chunks of ore that filled the barge.

They were rushing on loud water again, through a narrow cavern; but this one was light. The walls were blue-white crystal. The water was milky white. Kemen's breath in front of his face was a cloud.

It was cold.

The stink was gone. The air, and even the barge, smelled clean and new. Crystal spears hung from the ceiling. Kemen struck loose a piece of one with the sword. It was sharp and bright, but while he held it in the palm of his hand it forgot to exist and became water, like the pony of Noese, as long ago as it was far away.

He grinned again and sheathed the sword called Wyrldmaker and curled up beside Maer Ash to sleep some more.

Their limbs grew lighter, and the air grew colder, as the barge rushed on.

"The mercies told me of this," Maer Ash said. "It is called snow." It fell in pure white crystals from the mist that drifted from the spray to the walls of the cavern. It covered the barge, the gray ore; it sparkled in Maer Ash's short red hair, which was growing longer.

She grinned back at Kemen as the barge rushed on. They had been to the wyrld's bottom and wherever they were bound, they could only be bound back.

The walls of the cavern receded and disappeared into the mist. The roar of the water dropped, and the barge stopped plunging and spun slowly, enveloped in a white cloud. They slept and woke again, lost in a cloud of white as total as the black under the wyrld had been. Still, they did not feel fear; they had no fear left to feel. Tired of staring at nothing, Kemen drew the sword and held it out before them. They could barely see the faraway blue light, shining like a city on a hill too high to climb.

They found each other with their hands and laughed.

It was Kemen who was sleeping when they drifted free of the mist. Maer Ash watched it fall away in patches, revealing deep green water; a towering wall of ice all kissed by clouds; the light-streaked sky and then ...

She woke Kemen roughly.

The sky was filled with wyrld.

The barge was drifting down a broad, peaceful river, and above it, floating huge and near, was an entire wyrld of mountain and grassland and desert and sea, forest and city and stone! Kemen could see white dots that might be creatures grazing on the yellowgreen slopes of a range of hills that hung down directly overhead. Far beyond, in one jagged corner of this overhead wyrld, a dot that might have been a ship sailed across a blue-white sea on a wind that Kemen couldn't feel. Between were icy peaks and corners filled with darkness or with cloud: the rough edges of a wyrld as ragged in shape as one of the ore lumps that filled the barge.

Kemen caught his breath, and then Maer Ash's hand. It looked as if this wyrld was about to fall onto them, and then as they stared, as if they were about to fall into it. But it didn't and they didn't. The barge drifted on smoothly between low banks crowded with sweet-smelling trees.

To one side of the wyrld overhead, and beyond it, was another wyrld. This one was all of water and almost round, like a teardrop clouds were clinging to. Beyond both wyrlds was the familiar light-streaked sky. Nearer and yet somehow farther away, in the exact center of the air between all three wyrlds, a blue light gleamed— shining with the same faraway light as the blue stone in the hilt of the sword called Wyrldmaker.

A pony paced them on the bank, and Kemen

could see the orange leaves of the forest through its body.

"Look!" Maer Ash cried. She pointed behind, to the mountains that towered over them, all ice cliffs and cloud and forest and high streaked stone. "We have crossed the mountains of Aer."

Their limbs were light and they laughed. Bright houses appeared on the bank. The river passed under a slender bridge, all of glass, and Kemen called out to the two children who leaned on the rail watching them with wide smiling eyes.

"What wyrld is this?"

"Why, Llamp!"

Ahead there was a city.

THIRTEEN

LAUGHING, THEY RACED UP THE narrow steep stair street, chasing each other, dodging the startled traffic of vendors and beggars and seekers, leaping long, easy offwyrlder leaps that drew stares even here, where every third creature was an offwyrlder. They were hurrying to meet the airship for Glidr, even though there was no hurry.

Llamp! Steep city of air and light, knifeport and wyrldgatherer, bright in the blue gaze of the shining wyrld between the wyrlds that Kemen had learned was called the Far By. Llamp was a city of stairs that all led up, toward the cloudhidden top of a peak in the center of a vast orange forest. There were no roads to Llamp, only river and air, but that was enough: the city was busy with offwyrlders selling stormwood, gold, hides, promises, ore, love, war, and precious iron.

Maer Ash pulled ahead, and Kemen quickened his pace to catch her. Flight was her favorite game. The street curved over a ledge, and above it Kemen saw the sky-filling plains and peaks of Ture. It was easy to imagine, in the limb-lightening air of Llamp, that he was running downward instead of up, falling toward the wyrld above.

But Kemen didn't like to imagine that, not even now, after several sleepings in Llamp.

He rounded the corner and ran into a crowd. The street was filled with Puino, the beings that called Llamp their own. Their useless wings fluttered happily as they rubbed one another's arms. The air was filled with perfume, for they spoke in smells and were agreeing. Kemen made his way politely through them and around another corner.

Maer Ash was gone.

"Here," she said, laughing. She sat on a low wall behind him, overlooking the wyrld. Kemen tossed a coin to a being that tossed him the bruise-blue flesh of a beast that grew flesh like fruit, and they shared it, sitting shoulder to shoulder, looking down across the shiny mica roofs.

Far below, beyond the mudflat and shanties of the knifeport where the river washed the mountain's base, beyond the broad ice-blue river, an orange sea of forest stretched all the way to the Mountains of Aer which rose like a wall against the light-streaked, distant part of the sky. High up the slopes, the forest turned red—deep as blood where it gave way to stone and then to snow; deeper still where it was split by the white slash of the glacier that spilled down the mountains and joined the river in a confusion of clouds.

"I never knew wyrlds to be beautiful before," Maer Ash said. Kemen nodded. She was beautiful too in her new robes they had bought with the ore that had stuck in his boots on the beach at the bottom of the wyrlds.

As if reminded of Maer Ash by Kemen's thoughts, an airship appeared from behind a cloud over the forest below. It was the one they were on their way to meet, for she was going to Coenti Jjl to the Learnwyrlding. Kemen's eyes searched the high slopes and found Glidr, the first stage on her journey, a tiny silver spot on the snow. It looked like a tear the highest peak had cried.

"Come on," he said.

The stairstreet ended in an avenue that circled the peak on top of a cliff half of walls and half of rock. The air port was halfway around. It was a crowded ledge below the avenue. Puino and people and slow-eyed frin were filing aboard a luxury liner for the voyage between the wyrlds to Ture. It was said that the journey took half a lifetime, but everyone on the ledge got on the ship; there was no one saying goodbye. The great ship was like a city in itself: a wooden web of walks and rooms, hauled upward by unseen honking beasts in dark bags on long ropes. As Kemen and Maer Ash watched, it pulled in its ladders and spun off slowly into the blue-lighted air. Passengers waved from the balconies.

The ship arriving from Glidr was much different. It was fast and sleek and bright red. It seemed even smaller now than it had when they had first seen it, moving across the high snow-fields like a drop of blood, from the window of their narrow room.

The room that had been just wide enough for them.

"Something's wrong," Kemen said. The airship was an open, boat-shaped craft held aloft by a bundle of stormwood logs.

"Nothing is wrong that is not supposed to be wrong," Maer Ash replied. She took his hand. Her leaving lay between them like a knife.

Kemen felt under his robe for the comforting, icy touch of the sword called Wyrldmaker. Something was wrong. The ship was coming in side-ways, very fast. The passengers sat perfectly still in straight rows, looking straight ahead.

When they had first seen it from the river, rising from the forest in a shining heap of roof and step and steep street, bothered by airships and clamor and cloud, bright in the blue air, smoky, loud, Llamp had looked to their eyes that were sore with the sights of wyrlds' ends as sweet as wyrlds' beginnings. Llamp! Where wyrlds meet and journeys end.

And Llamp had not disappointed them.

They had come ashore at the foot of the mountain, leaping to the crowded street just as the barge was being nosed into a cavern loud with fires and ringing iron by ropes hidden under the water. At first they were afraid, remembering the trap in Aer; Kemen clutched

Maer Ash's hand and they edged against a moss and gold wall, starting up the street away from the river, trying to look inconspicuous. But how could they be otherwise? The street was filled with wyrlders and outwyrlders, beggars and children, warriors and skysailors, shouting and hurrying arm to elbow to wing. None had time to notice a filthy king and a hungry bride of the dead just arriving from under the wyrlds where no living being had ever been before.

Their limbs were light and climbing was easy. They had never seen such a variety of buildings and beings. Stairways and ladders and tunnels and arches and windows and walls crowded the crowded streets. Doors of all shapes, rooms of all sizes, mud and wood and gold and glue; blood-red reed shacks leaned against palaces, and half-finished, half-ruined towers rose between. And here were all the beings of all the wyrlds. Some were tall with chitin faces, some were short and fast, some loud, some wet with sweet fluids. The street as they climbed was thronged with web and wing, flesh and scale, hoof and fur and hand.

"Llamp!" Maer Ash laughed. They leaped up the street, their fears gone.

Halfway up the peak the slope grew steeper and the streets turned to stairs. On a narrow ledge in a three-walled building a pot boiled, and Maer Ash found that the ore stuck in Kemen's boots and in the pockets of her robe could be traded for sweet soup and a clear drink that was like icy water with fire swimming in it. They sat and looked at the streets below, at the river that separated beyond Llamp into a thousand tiny streams under the orange leaves, at the looming nearby mountains of Aer and the sky filled with wyrlds upside-down.

"You are from far away," said a deep voice from behind them. Maer Ash jumped to her feet and Kemen reached for the sword called Wyrld-maker hidden under his robe, and turned . . .

It was the horse-headed throndy that had served them their soup. She was smiling; at least Kemen supposed it was a smile. She sat down between Maer Ash and Kemen at the table on the edge of the cliff, holding a steaming drink between her one large and her one small hand.

"I know by how filthy your robes are. How scarred your faces. How big your eyes," she said. "Every being here is from far away. Knowing it is like knowing nothing."

Maer Ash smiled. They both relaxed, realizing they had spoken with no beings but enemies since the Cities of the Well.

The throndy pointed to the rolling plains just overhead. "I am from Ture," she said, "where this wyrld is called Sky. The other, all water, is called Mooon."

"And the other?" Kemen asked.

Kemen pointed to the blue light in the sky between the wyrlds. He didn't like looking at it; it chilled his eyes but held them like the stone in the hilt of the sword called Wyrldmaker.

"That is the Far By," the Throndy said. "It is not a wyrld but a watcher of wyrlds. It is said to be the eye of the wyzrd that lives at the top of Llamp, in a great castle hidden always in clouds."

She had just told Kemen what he had wanted
to know but had been afraid to ask.

The throndy loving to talk, Kemen and Maer
Ash learned that they loved to listen, sitting at
the narrow table with the soft, mumbling beast
between them. They learned that all the wyrlds
they knew—the plain and the rim, the Treynes
and the wyrldwall, Llamp and the mountains of
Aer—were one wyrld called Wen, which was a
spinning lump of corners and crevices and seas
like Ture, only slightly smaller. Maer Ash
learned that Coenti Jjl and the Learnwyrlding
was two journeys away: one by airship to Glidr,
and another on a draggon across the airless
passes of the Mountains of Aer. They could see
Glidr from where they sat. It was a tiny silver
dot at the high edge of the snow, near a cleft in
the peaks.

Kemen didn't ask of Noese, or show the sword
glowing at his side beneath his cloak. He had
grown wise. He watched the clouds swirling
around the peak at the top of the city. He was
going directly to the wyzrd this time.

The throndy gave them a narrow room and
they slept, then went to a robesmith on the street
who shook the ore stones from Kemen's boots as
if they were bugs and he were hungry. But it
didn't matter. They weren't in Llamp to make
their fortune. Kemen looked more like the king
he had refused to be with his robe cleaned
shining white, and Maer Ash looked almost like
a queen in a new rose tunic with a rack of new
knives across her breast.

133

They felt foolish, parting, if only for the brief while.

"I go to seek the wyzrd," Kemen said.

"And I, the Learnwyrlding."

They agreed to meet back at the throndy's inn. Kemen started in long steps up the stairs toward the clouds that hid the top of the peak. Maer Ash started down toward the air port.

As Kemen climbed higher the streets grew less crowded. The buildings were farther apart, and there were weeds and stones between them. His fingers brushed the cold hilt of the sword beneath his robe and he smiled. The wyzrd waited not far ahead! And Noese. . . . The clouds gleamed in the blue light and his journey sang through his bones like wind. His step quickened.

The stair became a trail, then leveled off and became a path. There were no more buildings. He was at the top. The clouds were a ragged wall of mist across a rough field littered with cut stones and stunted shrubs. There was no wind but the clouds rolled gently, as if powered, breaking off and floating away into the air. A chill finger of mist brushed across Kemen's face and he felt a strange desolation.

Clutching the sword under his robe, he walked into the wall of cloud. It was dim and he could barely see his hand in front of his face. He felt lost, uncertain, and he slowed. Tears came to his eyes. He took a few more steps and began to cry; he fell to his knees, choked with sobs. Kemen had felt fear before, but this was worse. It was an anguish more painful than anything he had ever felt. It was not fear but the thing itself: a sorrow too deep to plumb . . . he fell backward and crawled toward the light, his lungs racked with moans for his son, Hayl, gone, his kingdom, Treyn, gone, Noese, gone, lost, all lost, lost. He was lost, the wyrlds were lost, and all was grief and sorrow. Lost.

He ran.

He found Maer Ash at the Throndy's table and, still weeping, fell into her arms. He told her what had happened and she comforted him, stroking his graying hair.

"Still, you must go," she said.

Kemen nodded. He sat up and dried his eyes, shrugging his great shoulders as if to throw off his cloak of sorrow.

"Yes, I cannot turn back now," he said, "but my heart is filled with wanting to. There is no happiness in this destiny I seek, but only sorrow on sorrow, I think."

Maer Ash nodded. "It is so with the Learnwyrlding also," she said.

"And still you seek it."

"Still I seek it. One must seek something. Look!" Far away, high on the slopes of the mountains of Aer, a small red dot was drifting across the snowfields below Glidr. "There is the airship that will take me to Glidr. I found out where to meet it and was told it will be here in a few sleepings."

"I will stay with you until you go, and then seek the wyzrd again," Kemen said.

He was surprised to see that she was weeping too. He put his big cheek against hers so their tears mixed; the Throndy brought them soup and they ate together while they watched the airship cross the ice. It moved so slowly and the wyrlds were so huge!

They paid for a narrow room and slept and then made what they discovered was love while the airship drifted across the lower slopes. They walked through the city and ate, laughing, and loved some more while it sailed across the orange forest below.

Then, when the airship was climbing on its final approach to Llamp, they went together to the air port to meet it.

It was a trap.

FOURTEEN

THE TWIN ROWS OF PASSENGERS IN the airship all looked alike because they were wearing masks: the noseless, faceless mercie masks Kemen had seen in Wellkeaper.

Two of them jumped to the landing as the airship drifted in; they secured it with ropes of skin and the others jumped across in deliberate, uniform, deadly ranks. There were half a hundred of them and each held a straight glass two-edged sword in her left hand and a glass shield in her right.

"These are the mercies of the Long Tooth," Maer Ash said. "They use not knives but swords. My beloved Been spoke of them with awe. They leave neither wounded nor bodies behind, only slices where whole beings were."

Kemen caught her arm and pulled her toward the stair that led from the air port to the avenue above: but the mercies were swift and already it was blocked by twice ten swords. Thrice ten advanced in a faceless wall from the ship, their long swords whipping the air.

"It is us they are after!" Maer Ash said. Kemen had never doubted it. He drew the sword called Wyrldmaker and held it high: the blue stone in the hilt shimmered in the blue light of the Far By, as if the two jewels were whispering.

"Hold!" shouted a chorus of familiar voices.

"Mone!" said Maer Ash.

"You!" said Kemen.

"Us," corrected Mone four times in unison from the bridge of the airship. He stood grinning in a hideous clump. Three of his bodies had drooling, unformed heads; one was older and more familiar.

"Mercies, let them lay down their arms and go," the Mones continued. "It is the sword I seek."

"Then die four more times!" Kemen shouted; and then whispered to Maer Ash, "Go, quickly!"

Her answer was a flying knife that buried itself in the neck of the nearest mercie, who fell screaming a spray of blood as Mone shouted, "Render them!" But his order was lost in the din of war. Kemen's sword had already begun to sing, leaving four pieces where two mercies had been. The rest danced back, and then began to circle, silently.

The air was a storm of swords. These were the legendary mercies of the Long Tooth, whose skill at making death was advertised by all the one-armed warriors who had met them on the battlefield. They were as magnificent as their legend.

And as dread.

Kemen's left arm was cut deep and hung useless, and he wielded the sword with one hand. A blade flashed by his head; his hair felt wet and he blinked back blood. Maer Ash fell back with glass in her thigh, then pulled it out and fought on until her knives were all gone, each buried in a throat; then she snatched a blade from the hand of a corpse and fought back to back with Kemen.

The sword called Wyrldmaker sang. How it loved to kill! In Kemen's hand, all numb with joy, it split heads, peeled flesh from bone, cut down whole ranks of mercies to shards of glass and hair and teeth. Kemen's huge calf was sliced almost from his leg but he fought on, enthralled by the sword's killing song. He crouched and sliced a body from its dancing feet, and left them still dancing in a little red sea.

But it was not enough. Five, twice five, twice ten mercies died, and still thrice ten were left. Their swords connected more often, and the blood at the feet of Kemen and Maer Ash grew deep as the blood in their bodies grew shallow. Maer Ash was weakening. Kemen's sword still sang but his body screamed with weariness. Maer Ash fell to her knees and Kemen pulled her up; he tried to run for the stairs but they were still blocked by masked warriors. He tried for the airship but it too was blocked. He slipped in the surf of his own blood and got up again, straddling Maer Ash where she had fallen; he slashed angrily while on the ship the Mones clapped their fat, unformed hands in glee.

"Hold!"

It was a different, a deeper voice this time.

A white-haired man with a gray beard stood at the top of the stairway. He was unarmed and wore a simple robe of plant fur as blue as the clouds that sometimes covered the Far By. He started down the steps, then stopped halfway as the Mones began to scream: "On! Take them! Strike!"

But the mercies had stopped in their tracks, surrounding Kemen and Maer Ash. Kemen, exhausted, lowered his sword so that the point rested on the blood-spattered rock.

The old man held up one huge and wrinkled hand and spoke. "Mercies! I call on your code."

As one creature the mercies all turned, laid their long swords down, and wheeled back around in one ritual movement to face the man on the stairs.

Even the Mones were speechless.

"Their code!" Maer Ash whispered, pulling herself up on one knee. "I've often heard of this, but never seen it."

"What?" Kemen asked.

"An auction," Maer Ash said. "No one owns the mercies. They are bound to sell their blades to the highest bidder, even in the heat of battle, when they are called to their code. But who is this stranger who would buy our lives?"

"Perhaps it's not our lives he wants," Kemen said. "You must know by now that there are many forces vying for this sword I bear." He said no more, but he hoped that the old man had been sent by the wyzrd.

"So begin," the old man said.

The Mones conferred. The mercies stood, quiet behind their masks, in the ancient ritual that few had ever seen. The silence was broken only by the dripping of blood from stumps, the whistle of air in punctured lungs.

The stranger was old but not bent or stooped. He looked to be about twice Kemen's age. His eyes were pale, as if they had once been blue, and his hands and face were marked with the scars time leaves as it passes through the lives of men like wind.

"I double my offer!" the Mones cried out, rocking the airship in their excitement.

"He speaks wrong!" the old man barked. He looked at Kemen, at the mercies, at Maer Ash, but never at Mone. His voice was harsh. "He is held to the ceremony whether he likes it or not. He must begin with a bid, not double something that is unknown to me."

The airship stopped rocking. The Mones sat down. The oldest spoke alone, in a voice less shrill and more familiar to Kemen.

"My price you laid down behind you when he called on your code. Blades. Blades that neither snap nor dull, blades that seek blood as lungs seek air."

"I double their number," the old man said. "Bending glass for mercies yet unborn."

"Mean!" cried Mone. "He but matches what I offered before. I'll match that, for I know the sea from which they spring, and add the wings to bear them to the flesh they seek; the airship on which I stand."

The old man laughed, and when he laughed

he laughed that wyzrd laugh. Kemen's hopes soared when he heard it. He smiled at Maer Ash and she smiled back weakly.

"As if war were a thing of things!" the old man said. "I'll give you the stormwood for a hundred ships, but more: a door to match death's own: the newborn of Llamp to fill your ranks with life!"

The Mones looked shaken but the mercies never stirred. They stood in stiff, straight ranks like the dead.

"All right, then!" Mone said. "Coenti Jjl is yours. Not just younglings but the oldlings too. The trade. The towers! Now take him. Take the hand from the arm and the sword from the hand."

The mercies stirred. Kemen felt fear, for the old man's face was ashen, as if he were beaten. But not for long.

The old man's voice was almost a whisper. "Stay," he said. "I can top his bid, and will. How grand is Coenti Jjl? What are babies but the makers of warriors, and what are cities but the makers of babies? I give you the maker of cities itself. Look around you."

The mercies stood stone still.

"The wyrld."

"You can not!" Mone looked for the first time directly at the old man, with a look of pure hatred.

The old man looked directly at Mone for the first time. "I can and will," he said. To Kemen he said, "Come," and started up the stairs.

Kemen sheathed his sword and helped Maer Ash to her feet. Together, they limped after the man who had traded the wyrld for their lives. Halfway up the stairs they were stopped by Mone's scream.

"Again you win," he shrieked in a single voice. "But only for a time."

Kemen couldn't tell if it was to him or to the old man that he called, but it was the old man who answered. He laughed that wyzrd laugh again and said, "A time is all there is."

"Look," Maer Ash said. The mercies were stirring again, stacking their dead into piles for burning, picking up their unshattered blades. They took the airship and lined up the Mones, and began slicing them, methodically into a hundred pieces.

"It is the penalty for losing the auction," Maer Ash said.

"Worse than that," the old man said. "It is the penalty now the wyrld will pay, for that auction cost dear. But come."

He started up the stairs again and Kemen and Maer Ash followed.

It was hard going, especially near the top where the streets gave way to rocky paths. Kemen and Maer Ash were both still bleeding, and they leaned on each other for support as they struggled to keep up with the old man.

Near the clouds he stopped and came back to help. "You are badly wounded." he said. His voice was warm; he put his arm around Kemen and walked with them more slowly.

"Who are you?" Kemen demanded. "You are no wyzrd, for I know wyzrds well."

"I am your son, Hayl."

FIFTEEN

I̲T WAS NOT TIME BUT GRIEF, KEMEN realized, that heals wounds; for when the three of them emerged, weeping, from the clouds into the light at the top of Llamp's peak he was no longer bleeding. The cuts on his arm and leg were long, red welts, but they were closed; so too were the slashes on Maer Ash's shoulder and face. Kemen's head was still sore, but it no longer filled the room at the back of his eyes with fire; it was as if the tears had chased the pain away. He blinked the last of them away and looked for the wyzrd's castle as they emerged from the fog at the top of the mountain.

There was no castle.

At the top of the mountain there was a stone tower no wider than a net-house, no taller than two men. It looked absurdly squat next to the castle wreathed in cloud that existed only in Kemen's imagination. There were no high balconies, no parapets or tiers of stairs. There was no Noese. There was a single step, damp like a pier, under a doorway with no door. Inside was dark swirling mysteriousness. They sat on the step to rest. Even Hayl seemed out of breath.

Hayl.

Kemen could see it now: in the turn of his hand, the cast of his eye, the line of bone that defined his jaw and brow. Whether it was himself or Noese he saw reflected there he couldn't have said, for he hardly remembered Noese and had almost never seen his own face, except when it was caught for an instant in a bright shield or blade. But there was something familiar about the old man.

His son. Hayl.

He sat beside him on the step and Maer Ash sat below them, on the brown grass. The clouds that hid the top of the peak from the city below did not hide, but only softened, the view from the top. The splendor of Llamp lay all around, looking almost peaceful in the blue light. The air port was empty. Two piles of corpses still smoldered, for the mercies always burned their dead, but the mercies themselves and the airship had gone.

Below the crowded stairstreets, filled with shouts they couldn't hear—below the leaning walls and windowed cliffs—the cold slow river rolled off into the forest that extended to the wyrld's steep edge on three sides and covered the lower slopes of the mountains of Aer on the fourth.

Above, Glidr shined like a jewel dropped in the snow. Above, the forests and fields of Ture loomed slowly turning in the air. Above, round Mooon watched like a baleful eye of water. Above and beyond them all, was the light-streaked sky Kemen had first seen from the top of the wyrldwall.

The clouds gave it all a softened and dream-like look, so that from the peak of Llamp all the wyrlds looked peaceful, as if they were only dreaming a dream.

And in the center of them all was the steady blue light called Far By.

"But you are older than I!" Kemen said.

"Time is like wyrlds," Hayl explained. "It is not one but many things, circling but not touching. Our circles cross again here. More than that I do not know, nor can, nor can you, for what we see is partial: only a moment at a time. The rest is to this moment what darkness is to fire. Do you know darkness?"

"We do," Kemen said. He told Hayl of their passage through the darkness that filled the wyrld under the wyrlds. As he spoke Maer Ash leaned against his knee, nodding and then smiling, looking at them both and then looking away at far Glidr. Her journey was off but she was content.

Hayl appeared to notice her for the first time since the war on the air port. "Is this, then, your queen?" he asked.

Kemen hesitated only for a moment.

"Noese is my queen."

Maer Ash sat up as if awakened.

"Hand me then the Wyrldmaker," Hayl said.

Kemen hesitated for only a moment—then pulled the sheath from under his robe and pulled the sword from the sheath and handed it to his son. Hayl turned it over in his hands inexpertly. He held it by the blade with the blue stone pointing upward so that it and the Far By seemed joined, like watching eyes.

"The Wyrldmaker!" Hayl said happily. "Long have I waited for this."

"And Noese?"

Hayl handed the sword back to Kemen, and nodded toward the Far By, waiting in the sky. "If you have ever imagined that she waits there, you have imagined rightly," he said. "Now come, I have much to show you."

He stood and walked through the doorway into the swirling darkness without looking back. Kemen reached for Maer Ash's hand but she pulled it away. She would not look into his eyes. He hesitated . . . then followed Hayl through the doorway.

It was as if he had stepped off the wyrld. Kemen was falling. It was dark but a bright dark that tore at his eyes. Terrified, he reached out and found Hayl's bony shoulder and steadied himself and blinked. He was not falling. Somehow they had turned around; they were facing the doorway again. Kemen followed Hayl out.

The steps were grown over with blue weeds. There was no city below. There was no below.

They were in a broad valley, surrounded by hills, in a sea of grass that rolled in waves in the wind. Kemen's limbs felt heavy and his head was spinning. The mountains of Aer were gone. The Far By still gleamed overhead but Mooon had moved halfway around the sky. The wyrld directly overhead was unfamiliar, rough and wild, with toothed edges like a boning knife.

"We are on Ture," Hayl said. "Overhead, you see Wen, and on it Llamp."

The toothed edge of the rough wyrld was the mountains of Aer; and spreading from them to another sharp corner Kemen saw the orange splash that was the forest; and in the center of it like a drop of smoke, the clouds that capped Llamp. The very clouds in which they stood, had stood . . .

Hayl reached beind him and slapped the cold stone of the tower. "This is where the wyrlds meet," he said, grinning through his gray-streaked beard like a child with a beloved toy.

"And Ture," Kemen asked, remembering the throndy who had told him and Maer Ash her mournful tales. "Are there no beings here?" For the grasslands were trackless and empty.

"There are, and one of them we will know well, for it is essential to our journey. But first, come. You must know our enemy."

Hayl went back through the doorway. Kemen paused. Behind him he saw a flying shape skimming over the low hills toward the tower. It passed over. It was a great bird with wings stiff like wood.

Kemen followed and fell again, but this time he clung to Hayl's shoulder and followed him out onto the step without opening his eyes. He didn't want to see the darkness again.

Waves broke over the step, and instantly they were soaked with spray. A wild, menacing, featureless sea stretched out before them to a flat horizon. They were on Mooon. The wyrlds overhead were farther away. Kemen could no longer see Llamp, only the corners and crevices of a wyrld that seemed far too wild to walk across. Gentle Ture filled half the sky, and the rest was the light-streaked gray of the sky beyond, seeming to shimmer now, as if they were closer to it. Directly overhead, as always, was the Far By.

Hayl's white hair and beard were plastered to his skull and face with the cold, sweet-tasting water. His eyes were wild with excitement. He was shouting to Kemen over the roar of the waves.

"You must know by now that we have an enemy!" he said.

Kemen yelled back: "Mone!"

"Not Mone! Mone is but the image of that other, and serves him, even as you and I serve Noese."

"Where is this enemy, then?"

"You can not see him, you can only see him seeing you! Hand me the sword!"

Hayl took it by the point and plunged the blue stone into the water for only a moment. He handed it back to Kemen.

"Watch!" he said.

Even as he spoke a wall of water was gathering, as tall as the tower. An eye as large as a small man's head appeared in it. Kemen started toward the doorway but Hayl held him back, and the wave washed over them.

"We are safe here," Hayl said. They both were dripping wet. "Mone is his hands and even though he knows we have the sword he cannot seize it!"

The eye was watching them again from the center of another wall of water rolling toward the tower. Hayl showed no sign of fear. He was grinning. He seemed to enjoy defying this enemy.

"Why does he seek the Wyrldmaker?" Kemen shouted over the wild roar of the water.

"He doesn't. Only Noese seeks the Wyrldmaker. He seeks its destruction. Contained in it is the destiny of all the wyrlds, that is all that I know. And like you, father," he laughed, "it is all I seek to know!"

The second wave broke over them, drenching them. The cold water tasted sweet like clouds. A third wave was gathering into a wall, and the eye regarded them thoughtfully from its deep curve.

"You speak of destiny," Kemen said. "Is this enemy not also part of destiny?"

Hayl shook his head. "Have you never split the head of a man?"

"You know that I have."

"What did you find there?"

"Soft brain."

"Imagine a brain as big as an empty room, floating in fat that is floating in water that is floating in space unimaginable and thinking."

Kemen thought.

"Big enough to understand destiny and therefore bigger than destiny. Wanting to change destiny. Winning over other beings through an evil understanding called the Learnwyrlding."

"The Learnwyrlding!"

"But come. The door between the wyrlds only goes one way, and we must return to Llamp before we can return to Ture and begin our journey."

The third wave was about to break when they returned through the doorway.

Maer Ash was gone.

Kemen's robe was dry and his hair was long like Hayl's when he walked out onto the step overlooking Llamp. He searched on all sides of the tower and called down into the mist but she was gone. Hayl's hair and beard were also dry. He sat down on the step to wait while Kemen walked around the mountain top, peering down through the mist; but all Kemen saw was wyrlds.

He left the sword with Hayl without a word and hurried down through the clouds, weeping, toward the city. He knew why she had gone. He had hurt her. And he knew where she had gone. To the Learnwyrlding. To the evil of his enemy. Perhaps if he could find her in time, before she found a way to Glidr and Coenti Jjl.

But it was time itself that was gone. When he reached the streets, Kemen realized what the beard that covered his face meant and why his son's face was lined with age. The doors that crossed the spaces between the wyrlds also crossed time.

Llamp was much changed. Kemen ran through the streets where he and Maer Ash had played and found them empty. The buildings were gutted and burned. Skulls grinned in doorways where brightwinged children had smiled. The mercies had taken their payment; the city had been traded for a sword. And the weeds growing through the ribs of the dead that lounged in the gutters showed that they had taken it long ago.

Kemen didn't stop running until he reached the cold ashes that had been the Throndy's inn. He sat on the familiar ledge and looked across the unchanged wyrlds, to Glidr high in the snow. It was still there.

What had she called him? Fool. He realized now why he had left the sword behind with Hayl. He had hoped to overtake her on the crowded streets with her green eyes and leave it all behind: the sword called Wyrldmaker and the bright eye of the Far By and the baleful eye in the sea, and Hayl and wyzrds, and dreams, and Noese. He had hoped to trade it all for the narrow room they had shared.

But there were no more narrow rooms and no more crowded streets and no more Maer Ash. He looked from Glidr to the Far By and realized that it had been more than his unkindness that had parted them. It was true; Noese was his queen, his destiny. It was his lover, Maer Ash, that he missed, but she was as bound to her Learnwyrlding as he to his Wyrldmaker, and all that he had really missed was their farewell.

So he said it now, aloud.

He started back up the hill. He no longer dreaded the clouds; his own grief held him like a friend. He wept, and there on the other side was Hayl, holding the sword out for him to take.

Hayl had known he would be back.

SIXTEEN

On Ture they built a fire. First they filled their arms with wood, scouring the walls of the dry canyons that etched the plateau below the tower, collecting armloads of brittle sticks and hauling them back into a huge pile.

Kemen had been surprised to return to Ture and find they were no longer in a grassy valley, but Hayl had assured him that it was always so. "Perhaps the tower moves from place to place," he said, "or perhaps an awesome length of time has passed and changed the look of everything. I have never known for sure. But it is always different. On Llamp's wyrld, Wen, it is always the same. On Mooon, of course, there is no way to tell."

Hayl was old and he gave out long before the pile was high enough. He rested while Kemen made trip after trip down the canyon sides, until the pile of wood was as large as the tower itself.

"Enough," Hayl said, finally.

Kemen dropped to the ground beside him, exhausted. "Why must we build such a big fire?" he asked. "Must this being we are calling see it from another wyrld?"

Hayl shook his head and busied himself breaking sticks. "Not a big fire," he said. "A long fire. Our friend must see it not from a great distance, but for a long time." He arranged five sticks into what he called a star, then lit them with a liquid dropped from a tiny bottle he wore on a cord around his neck. "Now watch," he said, sitting down crosslegged in front of the fire.

Kemen watched. . . but his arms were tired from the armloads of wood; his legs ached from the steep canyon walls. He fell asleep.

He awoke with a start, leaping to his feet and clutching for the sword called Wyrldmaker under his robe, for looming over him was a great beast! Then he relaxed. It was the bird he had seen on his first visit to Ture. It was gazing into the fire with its rows of eyes and talking to Hayl in a low voice.

"This is the sCrib," Hayl said, whispered to Kemen. "It is the only being, besides the draggons that fly the high passes in the mountains of Aer, that is able to make the flight to the Far By."

"And it will take us?"

"We will see." Hayl put another stick on the fire to replace one of the five that had burned away.

". . . even as time and chance would tell, when my vision of my role in sky and wyrld was lost, and wind had given, unknown to others, to my wings alone a . . ."

The sCrib droned on, staring at the sky and the fire, talking of flight, and time, and luck in a low mumbling voice. It was the size of a small airship. Its stiff wings, which drooped in the dust beside it, were covered with silvery feathers, each one as large as a door. The wings were as beautiful as the head was hideous: an eyeless, furless, featherless bulb at the end of a stalklike neck decorated with four sets of lidless eyes. In the front of the head a wide mouth mumbled; it had sharp lips and no teeth.

The sCrib talked and talked and talked. Kemen fell asleep again, and when he awoke his bones were sore from laying on the ground. The firewood was almost half gone. Hayl was still tending the tiny, five-sticked fire, his shoulders bent with weariness. The sCrib was still talking.

"or at least seemingly so," it said, "for it is surely the most essential elements to existence that is to non-being the most peripheral, and therefore, just as the millkie dies in its own egg, the other beings that . . ."

Kemen fell asleep again. When he awoke the wood was two-thirds gone, and the sCrib was still talking.

"We're getting there," whispered Hayl.

"Getting where?"

"What he has to ask of us in return for passage to the Far By cannot be asked directly, but must be approached through a long discussion."

"unusual only insofar as my other plans, made long ago and never, really, understood, even by the one that . . ."

Kemen fell asleep again. When he awoke Hayl was shaking him by the shoulder. The sCrib was asking the favor it had come to ask. The woodpile was gone, and Hayl stirred the charred sticks, trying to keep the dimming flame alive.

". . . essentially is this," the great bird said, "that I would like to taste, not eat entire of course but only sample, as it were, call it curiosity if you will, which I cannot do without your help, if you would be so kind, my own brain."

The sCrib shut up. Hayl nodded to the bird, then nodded to Kemen. "The deal is one."

"What are we to . . ."

"Do not talk of it but do it," Hayl said. "Just what you would think. And quickly."

Kemen walked up the wing of the bird and climbed the neck. The head was covered with soft, wrinkled skin. He looked down and Hayl nodded. He drew the Wyrldmaker and sliced off the top of the head with one stroke; a disc of bone fell to the ground and rolled away in the dust like a wheel.

The sCrib gave a shudder but didn't speak.

"Go on!" Hayl said.

Kemen reached down into the skull and pulled out a handful of hot pink stuff. He held it down in front of the mouth. The sCrib gulped it from his cupped palm, then licked his fingers, one by one by one.

Ture was not all valleys and plateaus. They flew across vast seas of milky white water and trackless forests of trees that smoked and trees that sang; once they passed over a burning city

and heard faraway screams, but that was the
only life they saw as the sCrib beat its way up
from Ture, down toward the space between the
wyrlds, where the Far By gleamed.

The great bird flew heavily, but strongly. Its
stiff wings were made for riding the stormlines
and upwinds of Ture, and they beat slowly,
almost reluctantly. The sCrib had to be coaxed
away from its wyrld but the coaxing was easy:
whenever the wings lost a beat Kemen reached
into the opened skull for another handful of
brain. After the first taste, the sCrib's hunger
was insatiable.

Down the high air they flew; down the steep
space between the wyrlds toward the still blue
clouds, until Ture was no longer wyrld but sky,
like all the rest. They slept and woke and slept
again; their limbs grew lighter, and they
wrapped their robes tightly against the cold
wind. They sat on the thin, bony ridge between
the wings and felt it grow sleeker and fatter as
the sCrib flew on, until they could warm themselves in the luxuriant fur-like down.

"You're feeding it too well!" Hayl warned.
"The flightmind lies deep in the brainmass, but
we must take care or the sCrib will become too
stupid to fly before we reach the Far By."

Down, down they flew. The sCrib made long
slow circles until it seemed that they were even
farther from the wyrlds that filled the sky
around them than the wyrlds were from one
another. But clouds brushed the wings. Between
them gleamed the Far By, bigger now: a faceted
crystal that both hurt and held Kemen's eye. It

seemed that they were flying faster, for each time it reappeared after passing behind a cloud it seemed noticeably nearer.

Kemen grew excited. He reached deep into the sCrib's skull and fed it a large handful. The long wings quivered with joy. Kemen sat down beside his son on the sleek, warm fur.

Hayl looked worried.

"We are almost there!" Kemen said excitedly. "And will she be waiting?"

"I don't know," Hayl said. He looked older and worried. "I've never been to the Far By. I've never seen Noese. And I am afraid for some reason, for the first time, that I never will."

They circled it, getting closer with each long swoop. The Far By was a sphere made of a thousand diamond blue lights. It was larger than all Llamp and a hundred times more beautiful to Kemen's eye.

Then he saw dark spots against the blue, crossing their path on another, swifter circle, closer to the Far By. Kemen whispered to the sCrib, fed it a morsel and they turned; but the spots turned with them, tracking them.

"Draggons!" Hayl said. "These are the beasts that fly from the highest slopes of the mountains of Aer."

They were smaller than the sCrib, but swifter. They had teeth on their wings and teeth on their feet. There were a hundred of them. And on the back of each rode Mone.

SEVENTEEN

THE SWORD SANG SWEETER THAN ever, so close it was to the source of its song. Kemen sang with it until his arms were sore with killing and the down on the sCrib's wide back was slick with draggon blood. And still they came! Their long feet slashed at the stiff wings of the sCrib. They were fast and the air was thick with them. Kemen slashed back at beak and wing until the very wind was foul with a spray of blood, but he couldn't break through the cloud of draggons that stayed between the sCrib and the surface of the Far By.

On the back of each draggon a naked Mone screamed, neither fighting nor shrinking from the fight, just screaming: still screaming as they fell in pieces through the air.

"More!" Kemen shouted, but Hayl shook his head and climbed down from the sCrib's back. He and his father had traded places for the battle, since only Kemen could wield the sword called Wyrldmaker.

"There is no more," Hayl said, as the sCrib turned away from the battle. With no brain, it had no heart for the fight.

"There is only enough for one more feeding, and the Far By is as far away as ever. They seek to keep us away until our sCrib is too stupid to fly, and then take the sword. And they are succeeding. There is but one handful left, and that is the part that remembers to stay in the air."

Kemen sank to one knee and rested. Twice they had tried, and twice failed. His eyes fell to the wyrlds below, then lifted to the Far By that was so near.

He stood up and wiped the bloody sword between two fingers. "You lose heart too soon, my son," he said to the old man. "We have one chance left and we will take it." His eyes searched the waiting cloud of Mones for the one that had stayed back from the fight. The robed Mone. The hooded Mone.

"It is useless to go for the Far By," said Kemen. "We must go for the throat of the Mone, for always there is one that directs the others, and when his blood has painted my blade . . ."

Hayl didn't hesitate. He climbed to the head of the beast and scooped out the last of the brain for the waiting mouth. The sCrib's eyes grew bright once again as it sucked at the last morsel of its mind. The horde of Mones looked up with a single idiot grin, each seeking to be the first to feed the sword called Wyrldmaker.

But this time they were disappointed. Hayl

whispered to the sCrib and it dove under the draggons, then up behind them, into the path of the one that bore the hooded Mone.

Kemen jumped. If he missed he would fall forever—

He hit running on the draggon's wing and the hooded figure turned, surprised, to find a blade against its protruding belly.

"Do you never tire of dying?" Kemen asked.

With its small hands, the hooded figure moved the point of the sword upward until it rested between heavy familiar, beloved breasts.

"Kill me here," she said. "Do not spit on your own blade your own unborn child."

"Maer Ash," Kemen said.

"Fool!" Hayl shouted, waving him off.

Ignoring him, Kemen dove into the cloud of deadly birds. With Maer Ash clinging to his back, he flew the draggon with his knees, slashing a path through the toothed wings with his sword, toward Hayl.

The sCrib was dead. The smacking of its lips was finally stilled and its wings were stiff. Its emptied skull gleamed like a washed bowl. Hayl clung desperately to its back, his head buried in the fur to avoid the draggons that swooped at him.

"Fool," Hayl shouted again. "Go back!"

Kemen pulled out of his dive and matched speed with the sCrib. Instead of falling it had locked into an endless circular glide, around and around the Far By. Hayl's back and one arm were bleeding, but it was not too late. Kemen cleared the air of draggons with a mighty slash of the sword called Wyrldmaker and reached down for his son.

Hayl shrugged off his hand. "Your plan failed," he said. "She cannot call them off."

"Come," Kemen said. "We still have a chance."

Hayl shook his white-haired head. His eyes were small with pain. "I can give you a chance," he said. "Go now, while they are busy with me. Do not betray Noese!"

"I'll not betray you either!" Kemen shouted.

"Then go! Bear the Wyrldmaker to its owner if you do not wish to betray me. Go!"

"He's right," Maer Ash whispered. "Look."

The draggons and their grinning Mones were all clustered around them in a cloud, waiting for Kemen and the sword to leave, so they could feast on Hayl and the sCrib. The way to the Far By was open.

"Farewell," Kemen said. He sheathed the sword and, with the pressure of one knee, began the long, slow, unobstructed glide toward the Far By.

"He was right," Maer Ash said after a long silence. "I could not control them. Their brains are worn smooth from so much dividing and there are so many that the original is lost. They no longer even know the sword. They only know eating and dying, just as the draggons only know killing."

"But it was you who brought them. To kill my son." Kemen looked back, finally. The sCrib glided on, surrounded by screaming Mones and snapping draggons. Hayl stood, screaming blood, and leaped. He fell, spinning in a long slow arc into the clouds, and Kemen remembered when he had thrown him with one hand across a hall so many wyrlds ago . . .

"It was I but not I, " Maer Ash said.

"Farewell, old Hayl!" Kemen cried out.

"It was the Learnwyrlding," Maer Ash said. "The mercies were washing the streets of Llamp with blood. I was fierce with rage at you, but I could not join them. The wyrld they had won they did not want; they did not kill for treasure, but only took treasure because it allowed them to kill. I escaped to Glidr, and crossed the mountains of Aer on a pass so high that the wind could not lift the hair on my head, to Coenti Jjl. It was there that I learned what I had always wanted to learn, and became what I had never wanted to be, even while our child was growing within me."

"My enemy," Kemen said. The Far By loomed before them and he slowed the draggon's glide. "What then is this Learnwyrlding," he asked, "that it turns lovers into enemies? That it killed my son?"

"No more than this: that what Noese seeks with the sword you call Wyrldmaker is the end of all wyrlds. I am sorry for your son. I am more sorry for ours. I am sore bitter that I failed."

The Far By was a round wyrld of blue glass lighted from within. They swept all the way around it, but there were neither windows nor doorways; nor was there any sign of Noese. Kemen brought the draggon down to within a hand's breadth, but it wouldn't land. It hovered, quivering, terrified, even though he drew blood from its neck with the sword. He gave up and jumped, his boots ringing on the shining blue surface.

The sCrib flew by alone on its dead orbit. The draggons had all followed Hayl.

Kemen's eyes softened as he looked up at Maer Ash, waiting on the back of the trembling draggon. In spite of himself, he still loved her and he almost smiled. "You are free to go," he said.

"Or stay?"

He held up his arms and she jumped down into them and they both disappeared.

EIGHTEEN

Hayl had been expected with Kemen and entrymass had been set for two. At gain the entire "outer" surface of the starship and the "inside" changed places for a portion of a millisecond with a blue-white flash that awakened a child asleep under a tree on the far side of a hill on Ture, startled an insect hunter high on the slopes of the Mountains of Aer and was seen as far away as the dark ocean floor of Mooon.

Existence has its own inertia and having "existed" inside the Far By, Kemen and Maer Ash fell on through in real time and found themselves kneeling, breathless, on a narrow bridge of light that curved around the inner wall.

They looked around them in awe. They were in a great empty space, bridged and crossed by strands of light and metal mixed. The inner surface of the sphere was a shimmering blue, but seamless, without the diamond facets they had seen from outside. It was cold and silent. At the center, in a smaller transparent sphere, a woman stood at a console of colored lights. She turned and looked up at them, then turned back to her instrument. She was naked.

Kemen's heart was pounding. A bridge of light appeared from where she stood, across the space to end at Kemen's feet. Another blinked out across the sphere.

Kemen backed away, afraid.

"Go to her," Maer Ash said.

Kemen reached for Maer Ash's hand but she pulled it away.

"Alone. Finish what you have begun."

She was as beautiful as ever. She turned from her keyboard of lights as he entered, and held out the same perfect hand that had helped teach his body to sing. Kemen started to take her hand in his . . . then realized what she wanted. He unsheathed the sword and handed it to her and she smiled.

"You have done well," she said.

"I have bad news. Hayl is dead."

"I know. Now watch." She pressed a key on the console and a curved wall behind her turned milky, then clear. Through it Kemen saw not the inside of the Far By but all the wyrlds, as if through a window from far away. They looked small against the light-streaked sky; between them, even smaller, a blue light gleamed.

"You see ourselves from far away," Noese said.

She held the Wyrldmaker by the blade and

twisted the stone. Instead of coming free, it went out like a light. It was black. Then she pulled the hilt and drew, from within the blade, a narrow rod of purest darkness. Kemen gasped: the blade itself had been a sheath! She tossed the old blade aside and held up the dark rod.

"Here," she said, "you see the Wyrldmaker. And here, the wyrldmaking . . ."

She held the rod pointing downward over the console and placed the tip of it in a tiny hole. She began to push it down, slowly.

Kemen felt a terrifying swooping in the pit of his stomach, as if a bird were within him trying to land. The floor under his feet was spinning. On the screen the wyrlds remained still but the light-streaked sky behind them was changing. The lines of light now had ends, and they shortened as the rod disappeared into the hold, growing brighter as the gray between them grew blacker and blacker. The hilt nested with a click and the lines of light were points of light, impossibly brilliant against total darkness.

"Stars," said Noese.

The swooping feeling was gone and Kemen felt a hand on his shoulder. He turned and saw Maer Ash. It was the second time he had ever seen her crying.

"It is done," she and Noese said, both at the same time.

"I am exactly what you see," Noese said, "but what you see is not exactly what I am. I am a being like yourselves, and I am here with you, but you do not see my many forms, nor would you wish to. What you see is a tape of what you wish to see—or rather, what Kemen wished to see once long ago."

Kemen blushed. What he had thought was love was an image of light! He sat at Noese's feet with Maer Ash beside him on the floor of the control room as the starship made its approach to the predetermined star: the round fire on the viewscreen grew larger while they talked, like a hole burning through black paper.

Noese was relaxed and friendly, now that she had accomplished the task she called the seeding of the stars. She wrapped herself in a shimmering cloth and sat with them. Kemen felt uneasy in his filthy, stained robe, and he was hungry, but Noese never offered any food.

Maer Ash seemed angry. She had wept only for a moment, then stared at the screen while Noese talked. Finally she pointed at the star that was filling the screen and demanded angrily: "This burning! Is this then how the wyrlds end?"

"Maer Ash . . ." Kemen tried to quiet her, but Noese stopped him with a gesture.

"What do you mean, child?" she asked softly.

"I mean the Learnwyrlding!" Maer Ash said. "I must tell you that I came here as your enemy, for though you speak of the seeding of the stars the Learnwyrlding speaks only of the destroying."

Noese's eyes flashed. "And what is death to speak of destroying! To see only destroying! Look instead at the wyrlding . . ." It was the first time she had touched either of them, and she took Maer Ash's hand in her cold one.

"It is you who are the fool, Maer Ash," she said, almost tenderly. "For life is more impossible than you could ever dream. There are universes beyond universes, galaxies vast and countless stars in space unimaginable, and it is all dead. Dead. Time is a closed universe and in all of it only once did life arise, one time on one wyrld in one galaxy, in one small stinking seawater pool. Once. It never happened before and it will never happen again. Never. Know you, child, what never means?

"Every being that ever lived was born in the scum on the top of that one stinking pool. You. I. Life builds life. That is what life is. So . . ."

She walked to the console and with a wave of her fingers changed the viewscreen to show Ture, and the wyrld of Llamp, and Mooon. Her voice was low, but passionate.

"What you call wyrlds are parts of wyrlds. Pieces of wyrlds. Piles of spore-bearing rock, and water, ice and air and fire from many wyrlds, held together and hurled through the not-space to seed new stars by the starship in which we ride." She smiled proudly. "Of which I am the captain."

Maer Ash nodded, but didn't speak.

"But why am I part of this plan?" Kemen asked. "Why must one king cross wyrlds, and fight and suffer so that life can pass from star to star?"

Noese laughed. "That wasn't part of the plan. It was my fault. I got lonely, and I left the starship. I sought a lover."

Kemen nodded and Noese shook her head at the same time. She laughed again. "No, not you!

One more my own kind, who could satisfy my own longings. Remember that what you see is not me."

She passed her fingers over the console again and the wyrlds on the screen were replaced by waves. An eye in a great gray face appeared, then dove.

"Nor is that me," Noese said, "but closer, in ways that only I need to know. You need know only that we loved. That in itself was not wrong, but I had abandoned my duty in leaving the starship, and now I committed an even worse crime: I told my lover the story of the wyrldmaking I have told you. It is a secret that no beings on the wyrlds must know. It is the Learnwyrlding, and he used it against me to try and stop the wyrlding."

"But why?" Kemen asked.

"I know why!" Maer Ash said. "It is the other part of the Learnwyrlding. It is why I am here. It is that the wyrlding means that we all die."

"Exactly," Noese said. "And without it, the wyrlds go on forever, endlessly, the way they are."

"But still you die," Kemen said.

"Yes." Noese switched the screen to show the star. It was larger. "But not all at once. And not so soon."

"Three wyrlds becoming one around a star is not gentle," Noese said. "A wyrlding is a hard birthing. Life will survive and evolve again, but few beings will survive the wyrlding. Only the simplest ones. It is all fire and storm!"

"I understand," Kemen said. "But how did

172

your lover try and stop you then? And where do I come in?"

"He stole the Wyrldmaker," she said. "Never mind how. I am ashamed. We had two sons, and one of the sons stole it back for me. I couldn't get back to the starship with it, not then, so we hid it in a sword and took it to the wildest, most remote corner of the farthest wyrld from him."

"To me . . ."

"And got you to carry it to the Far By. My one son helped you, as best he could. He is called Wyzrd. The other found out too soon and tried to stop you."

"And he is called Mone," Kemen said. "What about Hayl?"

"I watched him fall," Noese said. "I knew him well, although he never saw me. Hayl was like the sword itself, part light, part mind, an image only and yet . . ."

"Hayl lived," Kemen said.

"He lived." For the first time she touched his arm and smiled. "I don't understand it, but we did somehow have a son."

"What think you now, Maer Ash?" Noese asked, getting to her feet. The star filled the screen and the lights on the console were blinking.

"I think it was wrong to try and stop the wyrlding. I would not try and stop you now . . ."

"You could not stop me now," Noese said. "For the starship's part is done when the Wyrldmaker is seated. The rest is done by the star. Already it is pulling the wyrlds together around us. It is almost time for me to go."

She changed the screen and it filled with fire and cloud. Ture and Wen were smashing together, violently but slowly, while Mooon broke over them both like a wave. Kemen imagined cities toppling and he could almost hear the screams.

"But how could we be in the center of all that, in the Far By, and survive?" Maer Ash said.

"We couldn't," Noese said. "Only in the not-space is the starship in the center of the wyrlds, and then it is only an illusion. Actually, I surround them." She began to study the lights on the console. "And I must begin my pullaway soon."

"What about us?" It was Maer Ash who asked. "Us?"

Kemen felt a chill. He found Maer Ash's hand.

"I return to the not-space, and where I go from there cannot be told to you. Nor can you go with me, for the mass would be wrong." She smiled abstractedly and turned back to the console. "It's too bad. You are pretty, both of you. Like the light on the waves."

Flying was hard. Maer Ash held onto the empty head of the sCrib while Kemen tried to hold the dead beast stable by walking from wing to wing. The stink was awful. The sCrib was mostly skeleton with just enough feathers clinging to the hollow bones to hold them in a stiff glide. Or perhaps it was the wind that held them aloft; it blew up from the storms below strong enough to fly a stone. Or perhaps they were falling and didn't even know it, for all around was cloud and smoke and darkness, lit by lightning from below.

Kemen gave up and clung to Maer Ash. They slept, they ate what rotten meat they could scrape from the wings; they flew on. Screaming as they spun through the wild air, Maer Ash bore their child, and they warmed it and she nursed it in their first rain.

They slept in one another's arms. Then Kemen awoke and found that the clouds were gone. He sat up, shocked by the stillness. Above was a sea of stars, and in the center of them was a blue light getting smaller and brighter at the same time: the starship completing its pullaway. While he watched it it was gone.

He looked over the wing. Below was a sea of clouds, dark in the starlight. The sCrib was circling toward them in a long, smooth glide. There was no wind but the air rushing by. Kemen lay down beside Maer Ash and tried to wake her, but she shrugged him away. He wanted someone to talk to. He had never felt so lonely as he felt looking at the sky empty of everything but stars.

They were asleep when the sCrib hit the water. Maer Ash clutched Kemen and they both clutched the child, but there was nothing they could do. It was dark. They waited. The sCrib didn't sink; its hollow bones floated it like a raft. The child began to cry, then found Maer Ash's teat. They waited, listening to the slosh of waves on bone.

A dim light filled the wyrld, even though they did not seem to be moving. They saw that they were floating near a rocky beach and waded ashore. Neither wanted to be the first to speak.

On the beach they walked. It didn't seem to matter which way. They passed a beached whale that was almost dead; its one eye was dim, dreaming, deeper than the dreams dreams dream.

They sat down on a stone. The wyrld was lighter still. Behind them a hill was covered with the remains of a shattered forest. In front of them was the sea.

Then at the faraway edge of it, they saw the strangest thing either of them had ever seen.

They saw the sun come up.